MISSION DOWN UNDER

Joan Embry

Publisher:
ASPG (Australian Self Publishing Group)
P.O. Box 159, Calwell, ACT Australia 2905
Email: publishaspg@gmail.com
http://www.inspiringpublishers.com

National Library of Australia Cataloguing-in-Publication entry

Author: Embry, Joan

Title: **ASUNCIÓN**/*Joan Embry*

ISBN: 978-1-922920-42-3 (Print)

ISBN: 978-1-922920-43-0 (eBook)

Acknowledgements

Our friend Allan Coatesworth (or George as I have always known him to be!), suggested that I write this, not just for my family as originally planned. He thought there would be interest in Sir Basil's second life after the Royal Air Force. He has encouraged me to keep going and financed the publication, for which I am very indebted.

Many thanks to his daughter Jane, who may have been roped in unwillingly, as she is an extremely busy author in her own right. She provided valuable assistance in the structure and setting out of this epistle.

Thanks also go to my very good friends Junette Case; Dot Carmody and Bev Hill (who have kindly proof read various stages of the manuscript) and Ken Hill who has given me valuable advice; daughter Jill for her expertise, and most especially to Donna Woodman. Without her I would have gone mad, thrown a brick at the computer, and consigned the whole effort to the trash bin! She has kept me sane, and patiently negotiated me through the intricacies of Microsoft, rescuing me so many times – "It has to be there – we'll find it!" - And generously spent her time advising and encouraging me throughout the whole business.

And finally my husband Mark, who has gently encouraged me to keep going and kept me straight on some aspects (he has his father's knack of being accurate when I was tempted to stray from or embellish the story!)

This book is dedicated to my own family. Our five children have shared our journey and now in the cold light of the 21st century some of our trials and hardships must seem unbelievable and perhaps even exaggerated. But over the years they have seen farming change so much; they have lived through the early years of mixed fortunes; so possibly some of the hardships do seem relevant and memorable to them!

I just hope that they feel as proud of their heritage as we do, appreciate the vision and hard work of their grandparents, and understand why they were in Australia and where they had come from. Another century; another country; a different way of living - but wanting and working towards a new life for themselves and their ongoing generations.

Our grandchildren are now of an age to appreciate the heritage of their grandparents – and now their children (our great grandchildren) are being born - and so life goes on!

"Per Ardua ad Astra"

Air Chief Marshal Sir Basil Edward Embry, G.C.B., K.B.E., D.S.O. & 3 bars, D.F.C., A.F.C.
Commander-in-Chief Allied Air Forces, Central Europe.
Photo by Elliot & Fry. (Permission of National Portrait Gallery, London)

Introduction

In February 1956 Air Chief Marshal Sir Basil Embry. G.C.B., K.B.E., D.S.O. (3 Bars), D.F.C., A.F.C., completed his tour as Commander in Chief of all N.A.T.O aircraft at the Headquarters in Fontainebleau Palace near Paris. He was considered by many of his World War Two contemporaries as one of the greatest war time RAF Leaders. He is the only RAF person ever to be decorated with the Distinguished Service Order four times accumulated by his gallantry in many periods of action during his service career. Aged 53 he would have had one more tour of duty and could then have looked forward to a good pension, possibly the odd directorship and a comfortable retirement for himself and his wife Lady Hope.

Strangely he completely disappeared from circulation and never returned to Britain. Most RAF Personnel heard nothing until about a year later when his autobiography Mission Completed was published by Methuen. This book outlining his 35-year career sold well in several editions and is a great read. He had previously cooperated with Antony Richardson to produce the book Wingless Victory. This is a detailed account of his nine weeks escape and evasion behind enemy lines after his luck ran out and he was shot down near St Omar France. Despite being captured twice he escaped and made his way back to neutral Spain near Perpignan, then to Gibraltar from whence he was flown back to Britain. Both books are available on the secondhand market.

Eventually we heard that far from a comfortable retirement Sir Basil, his wife Lady Hope, his sons Keith, Mark. and Paddy, plus Mark's fiancee Joan Bright, had all settled in Western Australia on one thousand six hundred acres of mainly virgin forest that they were going to turn in to a sheep farm. They were all developing the land and living on Sir Basil's pension till they could make it pay.

Mark married Joan after two years. They had known each other since they were fourteen and met when RAF children. Joan's father was the Wing Commander Aviation Medicine at the 2TAF Head Quarters in Germany, eventually to retire as Air Commodore Edgar Bright AFC. He was first a doctor learning to fly at Aberdeen university. He joined the RAF when the war started and later concentrated on altitude medicine and was awarded the AFC for his work with oxygen equipment at high altitudes in American bombers.

Mark and Joan now long retired decided initially to record a firsthand account of their life in Australia with Sir Basil. Initially this was for their ever-expanding Australian Family. However, they have decided to also publish their story which should appeal to a wide range of readers.

For his long service in many theatres of war Sir Basil received many honours and awards which were:

- Knight Grand Cross of the Order of the Bath.
- Knight Commander of the Order of the British Empire.
- Distinguished Service Order with three Bars.
- Distinguished Flying Cross.
- Air Force Cross.
- Mentioned in dispatches on four occasions.

- Commander of the Legion of Honour. (French)
- Croix De Guerre. (French)
- Commander First Class of the Order of Dannebrog. (Danish)
- Grand officer with Swords of the Order of Orange-Nassau. (Netherlands).
- This outstanding group of medals sold by auction at Spinks after his death for a record £155,350.
- G.A.C.

Contents

Photo Index

The Book

I had been thinking for some time that perhaps I should write down about the establishment and happenings of 'Ardua" (the farm pioneered in WA) as a record for the grandchildren and great-grandchildren to have. Like many good ideas it had never got past the thinking stage! I wanted our family to have more of an idea of Dad's depth of character, of his belief in what he was doing, and what he wanted out of life in his retirement for himself, his wife and family that he had brought out to Australia. Our children knew him as their grandfather, and he was very much loved and respected. As they got older, they read about him and his achievements and exploits during the war but perhaps did not fully appreciate how he wanted to continue to be challenged in life, and in his commitment to the dynasty that he was starting up in Australia. The narrative is interspersed with tales and accounts that highlight his service life as well. This helps to explain the type of man he was throughout his life, as a pilot and leader of men and as a farmer and leader in peacetime.

He did not speak much about his wartime days, but his strength of character and abundant leadership qualities are evident through the books. His farming character and achievements were the result of who he was in the Royal Air Force.

George, a good friend of ours, in the UK said to us why don't you write a book about Sir Basil's second life? After retiring from the RAF in 1956 he, with his wife and family, had moved from the UK to New Zealand to sheep farm, but as far as most people knew he had disappeared off the face of the earth, and they had no idea where he now was!

Our friend said there was still so much respect and interest in Dad's Air Force career and so many people wanted to know what had happened to him, with the strong belief in his continuing ability to still be making a difference somehow and somewhere. Dad had always had this retirement goal in the back of his mind. He certainly had no intention of settling in England because of the climate and possibly because he felt hampered in so many ways in the UK. He had always thrived on a challenge so the peacetime one in retirement had to be a good one. Pioneering an un-cleared area of virgin land in Australia to establish a sheep farm, whilst still leading a group of committed people - us! - seemed attractive to him!

This friend of ours was an ex-RAF pilot and he said there would be a lot of interest in RAF circles as Sir Basil's leadership qualities in light bombers were taught as an example in service training. He was involved in the formulation of the aircrew training syllabus after the war. A notable new part of the training was" escape and evasion exercises", based on his own experience. Useful for any airman unfortunate enough to be shot down and captured over enemy territory.

We remembered how on one of our visits to the UK in the 1980s we were staying with a very long-time friend with RAF connections in Chichester and she drove us to Tangmere for us to see the RAF Museum there, run by previous RAF personnel officers and NCOs. We greatly enjoyed looking at the aircraft and memorabilia there and all the mementos of the previous days of glory on this active wartime RAF station. When the retired Air Force people there saw Mark's surname as he signed the Visitors' book there was huge excitement and talk of the previous days of glory during the war under Sir Basil's command. We were quite overwhelmed at the huge regard, affection and remembrance displayed with such loyal and heartfelt reminiscence. When our friend returned to pick us up in her car the twelve or so gentlemen stood to attention and saluted as the car drove out. It was such a moment of absolute spontaneous loyalty and affection that left us choking with emotion as we appreciated just how much he was still held in high regard. And so the proposed idea of a book was strengthened and has born fruit.

Mark, my husband, has been beside me all the way with his memory of events. He has tempered my over-enthusiastic memory with his adherence to detail and the accuracy about some events. We have compiled this book of basically our memories and from our own family perspective. Obviously in the farming partnership there were the other family members, and we were all in it together at the start during Dad's lifetime, but basically this book is from the Mark Embry family perspective.

Dad's life and service career has been well documented in his autobiography "Mission Completed" and in the book about his escape from German hands after being shot down over France in the early stages of World War II. "Wingless Victory" (written by Anthony Richardson) describes his tenacious and aggressive character very well. Another book entitled "And the Walls came Tumbling Down" (by Jack Fishman) gives further insight into the character of the Basil Embry whose dynamic leadership was so well-known. This book was about the low altitude raid by the RAF Mosquitoes on the Gestapo prison in Amiens to release imprisoned Resistance members, and these Mosquito raids and methods used were the brainchild of Sir Basil. In the book Fishman spoke of the "Basilisation" that occurred when people became involved with or flew under him, principally because he would never ask something of anyone that they knew he would not be prepared to do himself and would never take "No" for an answer from the top brass and government ministers.

I suppose this was the charisma that we were instinctively drawn to at the beginning of our farming venture. What I am trying to say is that Dad's charisma and personality were the enduring attraction to the pioneering journey we set out on. Although there were many hardships, mistakes and successes, and years of privation as seen through realistic eyes - over the passage of time - we had many satisfactions and rewards and for us the farming life was a great one to bring our kids up in. I always fall back on the phrase "it was character building" and probably that came about because of the influence of Dad's leadership and belief in what we were doing.

And right beside Dad was my mother-in-law - Hope. She was a staunch supporter of Dad in his new life of retirement. She of course understood the huge challenge Dad was facing in settling down in a new environment away from the flying one that he had loved and had felt so committed to over the years. She realised he needed new goals to aim for and new difficulties to be challenged with and couldn't just settle for half measures or an easy life.

This meant great sacrifices on her part, as she moved so far away from friends in the UK and Europe. She had lived through the war with many uncertainties in those days, and so peacetime must have seemed very precious to her. Life in the RAF after the war as the wife of a Commander-in-chief entailed a very nice home to live in. It also entailed a cook and servants, a tennis court and a social life with a lot of entertaining of important visitors. As the wife of the Commander-in- Chief of the Allied Air Forces Central Europe, living in France at Fontainebleau there was a lot of international entertaining. Hope was an excellent French linguist, and she would have enjoyed her ability to converse in two languages and meeting so many people of different nationalities.

Imagine the contrast Australia. At the beginning, sleeping. on a camp bed under the stars and cooking on a methylated spirit stove outdoors, using kerosene (paraffin) and Tilley lamps, with no running water and working domestically under huge difficulties and challenges. She also worked like a navvy in the heat and dust out in the paddocks, clearing the bush and burning up timber, stumps and roots.

Only a very special person with a huge love for her husband, a loyalty and acceptance of duty and a very great understanding of his needs could have adapted to such a life. But adapt she did – indeed she embraced this new way of life wholeheartedly.

Mum's strong sense of duty would have been instilled in her at a very early age. Her father was a British naval captain attached to the Australian Navy helping in the formation of that service in Australia. He then became the Resident on Norfolk Island and she was brought up there for some of her childhood. She was the seventh child of a seventh child but always pooh-poohed the superstition that she must have psychic powers because of that qualification! She was always far too matter of fact and practical about life to entertain such thoughts or ideas!

She had one older sister and four older brothers. She lost two of the brothers with the Anzacs - one at Gallipoli and the other at Passchendaele, both in unmarked graves. Another brother had his eyes badly affected by mustard gas, in the First World War. She was then to lose another brother in the Second World War when he captained a destroyer which sank the German battleship the Bismarck but then sadly was sunk by a lone German bomber returning from that raid. How lucky was she not to lose her husband on one of the many bombing sorties he made over the Continent during the war?

So perhaps it was not so surprising that the Embrys ended up in Australia when you consider these very strong Anzac connections.

Early Wartime

It may be hard for the modern generation to appreciate just how desperate those early days of World War Two were for the island of Great Britain. Invasion by the Germans was a very serious possibility, as they advanced across Europe and occupied France. The English Channel was such a very small strip of water to be crossed by the enemy and it became more and more likely, as the Battle of Britain air war raged in the skies above. It was not common knowledge at that time, but the convoys of ships bringing food to the inhabitants of the British Isles were being pulverised and sunk by the German U-boats marauding the oceans. At one stage the reckoning was about fourteen days of food left for the inhabitants of the British Isles and then they would have had to surrender and be occupied by the enemy. The fighter aeroplanes in the skies above England were dwindling in numbers to keep the enemy at bay. Children were being sent to host families in safer areas to be looked after. Their mothers worked in factories or joined up in the Army, Navy or Air Force - all to answer the desperate call for man and woman power.

Hope had a knowledge of Russian and spoke fluent French and thought she might have proved useful as an interpreter but was not required in that role and so she joined the WAAF. Her strong sense of duty to the country in those desperate early days of the war meant that the four children were billeted out in Somerset with a family of three spinster sisters. This must have been quite a shock to the spinsters!

Hope served at Biggin Hill at one stage and Dad was quite worried when she was there as the airfield received quite frequent pastings in air raids by the Germans. She was also on the same RAF station as Dad once, indeed he was her boss. One day he had a friend working on some details with him in his office. Apparently, he said with a grin "watch this "and pressed a bell. A very smart WAAF officer came in, stood to attention and saluted. Dad then said, "that will be all Embry", but he made the mistake of speaking before the door quite closed as he said, "I bet you couldn't do that with your wife!" Very typical of his sense of humour! But I imagine Dad fairly copped it when he got home that night!

New Beginnings

The vision of England, with its neat little fields, hedges and greenery spread out below, as seen from his aeroplane cockpit as he flew operationally throughout that Second World War, must have been indelibly printed on his mind. This is what he had held dear and had fought to protect for so many action-packed months and years. The victory that had seemed nigh impossible at the start, as the might of Germany had so nearly crushed the desperate and dwindling resources of the Royal Air Force in the Battle of Britain. So many of his friends, fellow pilots and crews were shot out of the sky and failed to return from the interminable flying operations over the Channel, right through to Germany itself, day after day, night after night. So few aeroplanes remained to take to the skies and defend this English countryside as the German Reich so nearly overcame the opposition and invaded British soil.

Then there were years of operational flying and leadership in the many theatres of war, with the increasing responsibilities as he rose to higher ranks in these different areas of command. All this must have seemed never-ending at the time, and yet perhaps have seemed quite unreal and unbelievable in retrospect.

His last peacetime appointment, where he proved very popular and well liked, was as Commander-in-Chief Allied air forces

Central Europe under Marshal of France A. Juin, the overall Commander in Chief of all land, sea and air forces based in central Europe. Marshal Juin was deemed to be quite upset when the decision was announced to retire Dad from that position and from the RAF at the early age of 54. At the end of the war his forthright character and steadfast belief in cutting out the bulldust, which had characterised his wartime exploits, where he had led from the front in the air and on the ground, was possibly deemed no longer politically correct to the powers-to-be, so they chose to give him early retirement. As he said - "in other words I was sacked."

Dad had always said that when he left the Air Force he would retire to a warmer climate and out of England. He initially chose Rhodesia and his eldest son Keith had already gone out there to reconnoitre farming opportunities et cetera. But Keith was very disillusioned with living and farming there as he said you virtually had to carry a big stick to make the locals work and for them to respect you "as the white man", and you also had to carry around a big bunch of keys locking everything away. Keith said he would farm in New Zealand (where his young sister Bridget had emigrated) or anywhere - but certainly not Rhodesia. Around that time Rhodesian troubles were accelerating, and it seemed a sound decision to move to New Zealand. Their only daughter Bridget had settled there, married a farmer and seemed to love the farming life, the climate and the future prospects for their children.

So, Dad chose to leave the country that he had fought for and flown over for such a lengthy period to embark on another mission and career with new risks and challenges, albeit not so dangerous and death-defying. Whilst his RAF career was ending, they went to stay with Hope's cousin Mickey in the south of France, where he started to unwind and work on his autobiography whilst catching up on some of the leave that was outstanding to him.

On a typically English grey afternoon in March 1956 their middle son Mark joined them to board the SS Port Sydney to travel to New Zealand to begin their new life. This ship was one of the Port Line vessels that basically carried cargo, but with twelve or so passengers well catered for and looked after in very luxurious quarters. I must admit I was glad to know most of the passengers were over 50+, as this eased my mind over a possible shipboard romance for Mark! The ship went round the Cape of Good Hope, calling in at the Canary Islands and then other ports on the way to Wellington New Zealand. Dad concentrated on writing his autobiography whilst Mark enjoyed the company of the young officers on board the boat. On reaching Durban the family had a few days onshore as cargo was offloaded and this allowed the family to catch up with one of Mum's brothers and wife who lived there, plus various friends. Everywhere they went they met up with a lot of Dad's wartime flying mates, so there was plenty of ribaldry and happy times. They also enjoyed sharing time with more of Hope's family when the boat reached Australia, offloading cargo in Adelaide, Melbourne and Sydney. Then finally they boarded another ship to reach their final destination in Wellington New Zealand.

On arrival the trio were joined by their eldest son Keith who was working on a farm in the North Island. They then enjoyed some time with their daughter Bridget and family who were share- milking on a dairy farm in the middle of the North Island. Mark got a job on a farm whilst his parents went up to Auckland and caught up with quite a few ex-RAF friends and acquaintances there. They were lent a house on an island in Auckland harbour and spent quite a few months there whilst Dad finished his book "Mission Completed".

During this time, they travelled around parts of the North Island, looking at farming properties for sale, with the intention of starting their family farming adventure in NZ.

One area they looked at on the Coromandel Peninsula was close to where their daughter Bridget was moving to, to farm on her husband's family sheep farm overlooking the Hauraki Gulf and Pacific Ocean, with islands dotted off the coastline. A most scenic and attractive part of New Zealand, very good sheep farming country with perennial pastures, very hilly and steep country suitable for sheep grazing, dairy and beef cattle, but with not much cropping potential.

This Coromandel area had too high a rainfall to run Merino sheep for wool production. The denser fleece of a Merino does not allow the skin to breathe so well, therefore the wool can tend to rot on the skin causing dermatitis and clotting of the wool, which is no good for the wool trade.

British breed cross bred sheep have more open fleeces so the dampness can dry out; and are basically run for meat production with their wool being a by-product, so this area was very well suited to this type of animal husbandry.

Possibly the attractiveness of wool producing sheep had always been Dad's goal, whether in Rhodesia or New Zealand, that meant sheep husbandry involving basically Merino sheep for wool production – rather than fat lamb flocks of mixed crossbred sheep. Merino wool had been worth a pound sterling for a pound several years before – and that was the sheep farming that he had always quoted as his aim in life.

He also had the feeling that New Zealand was too reliant on agriculture, not having many alternative sources of income at that time, such as manufacturing and mining, and so he was concerned about the ongoing economy of the country as a whole.

The truth be told Dad was so unsettled in that first year one wonders if he had gone to Australia first, would he then have moved on to New Zealand? Small wonder, as he missed the Service life so much. There was also the sudden relaxation of the pressure that he had been under for so long, during the war and in his high-powered appointment with AAFCE. However, they did discover quite a few of their Service friends were living in or near Perth, WA and so it probably proved to be the right decision in the long run.

The Mediterranean style climate that West Australia had to offer had always been a drawcard for him. Perhaps the promise of untamed acreages in WA was the real drawcard for him more than the smaller acreages, steep country and mountainous vistas of the New Zealand terrain. Perhaps his first impression of New Zealand as he drove away from Auckland was to see quite a similarity to England in the countryside with many English type trees, bushes and vegetation and this may have seemed a trifle stifling to him. But basically, it was the price of the land in New Zealand that proved too expensive for his budget.

It certainly proved an expensive change to his plans as all the packing cases of furniture; his car and Keith's car had to be loaded onto a ship again and transported to Western Australia, accompanied by Mark and Paddy. There were storage costs for the packing cases in Australia plus the airfares for the two of them and Keith. All these costs would have made quite a dent in the eventual budget for their new life in WA.

State of WA

It is only in the later years that we discovered the length, breadth and variations in climate, fertility and clearing of this huge State as our own family expanded and extended their interests and livelihoods throughout the State and Australia. A brief synopsis of the State of WA may give the reader a snapshot view of how big and varied this one part of the continent is.

WA covers a large area of the map of Australia - from top to bottom, bounded by the Indian Ocean on the Western seaboard and desert on the East side. At the top of the map is the Timor Sea and down off the South of the State are the Southern and Indian oceans which actually meet off the coast of WA at Augusta, which seems quite mind blowing to me.

The climate varies from top to bottom, as does the terrain and productivity of the land minerally and agriculturally speaking.

The North and North-west of the State is bounded by the peacock blue ocean with great tides; a land of red rock and mountains, dry and arid; a huge emptiness of stunning colours by day and clear skies with millions of stars covering land and ocean in the darkness. Big rivers flow in the North-west and the country is well known for the cattle of the Kimberley. A land of aboriginal tribes, indigenous stockmen, and pioneer station owners. Cattle graze on hardy spinifex, but also on the grazing areas on station country adjacent to the big river systems. The mighty Ord has been dammed and a huge quantity of water flows out of this river into Lake Argyle. A tiny wall was built between two mountain peaks to flood this huge area of hills and valleys with water which then flows down by gravity into Lake Kununurra to flood the fertile soils South for agriculture. A magnificent feat of engineering creating fabulous vistas of red rock and hills, but with fertile soils and abundant water flowing down South, and East over the border into the Northern Territory. Crops such as cotton, sugar, chia, soybeans, chickpeas, and sweet corn are irrigated by gravity in these areas. Cattle and sheep for wool are also a feature of this country.

Travelling south are the massive mountains of iron ore of the Pilbara – so much a part of the wealth of the State of Western Australia nowadays. The Hammersley Ranges are a major part of mining in the empires of the Hancock and Forrest families. Gold mining also adds to the mineral wealth of the State, and I wish that Mark's parents had seen some of these parts of WA, as we have been fortunate to, as the whole scene accentuates the vastness and beauty of Australia and the colours of the landscape against the vivid blue sky are unbelievable.

The middle section of the State is flatter but still vast with wheat grown on huge tracts of land, basically cleared in the middle of the 18th century onwards. This area provides another of the major sources of income for the State, with wheat, barley, lupins and canola being grown. This region is very reliant on when the break of season comes and how much rainfall there is. However, there are many varieties of wheat and barley now that can grow in minimum rainfall to spread the window of their cropping and harvesting operations. Sheep and cattle also graze these areas, but the basic income is gained from cropping and due to the small window of opportunity for preparing the land for such crops the farmers run huge machinery keeping the operations going day and night.

Then leaving the station country with its large tracts of wheat growing and cropping areas and coming down further South to the area surrounding Perth, which is the original river settlement in the State, are smaller more intensive, irrigated landholdings with dairy cattle, and sheep.

Further South on the map of WA is farming country with higher rainfall and therefore bigger timber to clear. This is where Mark's parents chose to buy 1,750 acres, approximately 200 miles south of Perth in undulating country, with big Jarrah and Marri (Red Gum) tree forests, and a lot of land already cleared and being farmed.

This seemed to them to be ideal country with an annual rainfall of 30 inches and with the Mediterranean climate the family were looking for. The stock agents assured them the district was well-known for the running of sheep, cattle and a certain amount of cropping, and the price was right as most of the property was uncleared!

Smalltime farming compared to the Nor-West cattle and sheep station country or the vast acreages of the wheatbelt country, but big in acreage compared to farms in the UK.

Travelling South and Southeast of Boyup Brook the timber gets less and smaller, and so is cheaper to clear, and that is why the family expanded its farming operations down South after a few years, but that was some way down the track.

Most of the population is in the Western and Southern seaboard of WA with agriculture and mining now driving the population growth internally within the State.

Choice of BOYUP BROOK

Dad and Keith flew over to look at various places on the market in WA, and Hope joined them to choose a very un-developed farm in the Boyup Brook area which was within their price range.

Boyup Brook is in the South-west of Western Australia, about 100 miles inland from the coast, and is very attractive undulating country. It is quite heavily timbered with Jarrah, Red and White Gum and Marlock trees, with ti trees (small bushes) and rubbish grasses in the gullies. The soils are basically a light loam with ridges, plus a heavier denser loam, of reddish and chocolatey brown colouring, with outcrops of granite rocks. This denser soil on the granite country is very fertile but does not drain so easily and the rocks are extremely hard but in some instances on the lighter country the ironstone could be crumbly and porous and could be cultivated with machinery. Spreading the ground with fertiliser improves fertility of the soils over the years and seeded crops, grasses and clover respond to the ongoing fertiliser treatment.

The chief reason that Rhodesia (as it was then), New Zealand and Western Australia were considered as suitable places to take up the second phase of Dad's life were that their climates were similar. They could be classed as Mediterranean climates, with lots of sunshine in the winter especially and with consistent rainfall. WA has a very temperate climate - pretty hot in midsummer but with a very pleasant winter. Boyup did not have many days in the summer over 100°F, with a dry heat and basically cooling down a lot at night. The annual rainfall, mainly in the winter (June/July/August) was 30 inches so the dams got filled and feed crops grew well. The only drawback was that we sometimes had frosts in the winter which curtailed the pastures and crops in their growing season. We even had a light covering of snow one year in June, which gave our eldest son the excitement and incentive to get out of bed in preparation for school in his first year in the primary class!

Boyup Brook is classed as a very "safe area "in which to farm. Not prone to droughts like some of the interior wheat belt areas of the State, or sticky and humid as in the North at certain times of the year. If you look at the map of Western Australia and see how far it is between Albany in the South and Wyndham in the North and realise that it takes 4½ hours to fly in a jet! You will have some idea of how huge WA is! From top to bottom!

Fire has been part of the Australian landscape since time immemorial. Many of the Jarrah and Red Gums have blackened trunks from flames which have run up the trunks of the trees over the centuries destroying the canopies, but when the rains come the trees start sprouting and looking green again. Most of the Australian bush is extremely hardy and recovers from such fires. Sadly, it can give the scene a very dark appearance, with the surrounding greenery proving rather colourless too as I was to find on my arrival.

Some fortune teller once told Dad that "fire" was in his DNA and that was possibly true when one thinks of the Blenheim light bomber raids over France and Germany and the many low-level Mosquito raids, he flew on during the war, and then the burning up of the clearing he did in Australia on two farms!

Possibly the sight of a whole hillside bulldozed and alight reminded him of those halcyon days during wartime raids.

However, Dad had had this dream over the years of "pioneering" and so purchasing a 1700 acre property, of which only 2 ½ acres were fully cleared, really appealed to him! About 400 acres of the rest of the property had a percentage of "ring barked" dead trees, with a pasture of sorts growing between, and then acres and acres of "virgin bush" (heavily timbered country needing clearing from scratch with bulldozers.)

The acres of dead trees, mainly Jarrah, Red Gum and White Gum had been semi cleared by hand in previous years when the pioneers had wielded axes and chopped a wedge of the bark away in the form of a ring round each tree, called ring barking or sapping. This then caused the tree to slowly die, dropping dead limbs to the ground below as the pathway to the roots had been slowly demolished. The denuded trees stood like white ghosts in a cemetery of skeleton trees with native grasses growing underneath and with the addition of hand-sown clover seed the farmers were able to run some stock (sheep or cattle) amongst the trees. Of course, when the tree had completely died after many years, thus falling over, it was easier to burn the logs and limbs to create more grazing areas. However, we were pushing them over with the bulldozer, as we wanted to clear the paddock of timber. This frequently caused the brittle trunks to break. Stumps then left in the ground had to be pushed out by the bulldozer, or else given a dose of gelignite to blow them out. This treatment made the locals chuckle as the big bangs sounded like the Second World War all over again and they knew where the noise was coming from and who was making it!

It was much cheaper clearing ring barked areas than bulldozing the green bush, so this is where the bulldozers started. The ring barked areas were also already fenced and had basically native grasses and some small waterholes that had been dug out by the pioneers. These held the winter rain and provided the stock with good drinking water. Therefore, these were the areas we put the bulldozers into first, pushing the timber into heaps to be burnt when the burning season opened in March, so that we could then top-dress fertilizer and improve the basic pasture there to run more wethers and increase our income.

During the winter we moved to various "green" areas of virgin forest that had been ear-marked for the bulldozers to knock down and push into heaps or windrows, to dry out during the summer and then be burnt up the following autumn, as soon as the burning season opened. The bulldozers came back again to keep pushing these heaps together, whilst we manually did the throwing in of the inevitable sticks and roots as the timber got burnt. A certain amount of this virgin bush was then to be cleared every year for quite some years, at a huge cost of course.

Fire was a very necessary part of land clearing and we learned to cultivate a big bare firebreak around the planned area at the end of the summer. This allowed us to light up when the timber was warm and dry with local farmers coming with their fire-fighting equipment to prevent the fire getting away. We were fortunate that the State Forest surrounded our whole farm. Many other farmers were bounded by cleared land on adjoining farms and so lighting up their clearing fires could prove slightly more hazardous as sparks could spread more quickly with more disastrous and speedy results through pastures. But people had to be able to clear and develop their land to provide a living for themselves. So, we all rallied to the cause to give assistance on the days our neighbours were lighting up, just as they did for us.

Adding to Dad's pioneering dream was the fact that the only habitat on the farm was a four- roomed wooden shack with a lean- to bathhouse tacked on one end. He had never done a course in building or brickwork as some Service people did at the end of their careers to prepare themselves for hobbies in civilian life. Another dream of his was to build a house and he ended up building three houses in his Australian lifetime, virtually with book in hand for the first one! A far cry from his wartime Service career - but applying the same vigour, determination and dedication as when escaping from the Germans as a POW in France in the early stages of the war or flying with his squadron in his Mosquito aeroplane. His motto was that anything was extremely do-able - just a matter of application!

In The Shed

Mark and his youngest brother Paddy, who was aged fourteen and still at school in Auckland, boarded a ship to Sydney and then a coastal ship for Fremantle WA, where they disembarked with all the packing cases, Dad's shooting brake and Keith's ute. On arrival from lush green New Zealand with its long vistas and rolling established grassy hills and Persil white sheep, Mark's initial reaction was one of horror. He was not impressed. All he saw was loads of the green forest (native bush), that was dull in colour, compared to the bright green they had left behind in New Zealand. Areas of ring barked trees stood ghoulishly, as in a cemetery amid long khaki- coloured dry grass, giving the whole scene an unkempt worthless look.

Initially the owner was still occupying the shack and so the family settled their camping stove under a big wattle tree and occupied their camp beds under the stars until the owner started to remove some of his belongings and machinery out of one of the sheds. Leaving the camp beds outside, the family moved into the shed and were then able to house a kerosene (paraffin) fridge up against one of the walls to shelter it from the wind which greatly helped as it was the height of summer in WA, early in the month of January. They created some semblance of order in their makeshift kitchen and could sit around the table on boxes for meals. They had invested in Tilley lamps and kerosene storm lanterns and so were able to extend their evening meals making life slightly more civilized!

The journalists who came down from Perth to interview the new arrivals couldn't believe their eyes, or ears, when in response to their question "What do you most look forward to?" Lady Embry replied, "A kitchen sink with running water!" It was to be a long time before that eventuated!

After a week or two the farm was taken over by the Embrys and they moved into the recently vacated shack and gave it the grand title of Buckingham Palace! A corrugated iron tank caught the water off the roof for cooking, kitchen use and the ablutions. The toilet? Well, that was a walk down the paddock, with a spade and roll of toilet paper, into the native bush which consisted of ti tree, Marlock trees, undergrowth and a salty creek named the Perup River (and it's on the map of Southwest Australia to that effect!) Plenty of natural bush cover and acres of room!

Water

Water was diagnosed in short supply for the stock and so various dams were completed by the bulldozers before the next rainy season. These dams were constructed with the blades of big bulldozers with big rippers mounted on the rear of the machines. The siting of these dams was decided on where they were needed but what we did not realise was that the obvious area of need we chose required scrutiny for the quality of clay to be incorporated in the dam walls for pugging together to hold water when the winter rains came. Most of the dam sites were okay, but one in a gully was found to have very salty water. Stock drinking from it would have tended to scour and not do well, so we eventually fenced this dam off from the stock.

Apparently, there was quite a discussion before I arrived in WA as to what names were to be given to the dams. Dad's idea was to name each one after an aeroplane, but the rest of the family vetoed that suggestion! So, the dams were named after well-known lakes around the world. The biggest dam was named Taupo and the salt one was Utah! Amongst others were Windermere, Victoria and Geneva. Eventually we fenced the paddocks around the dams and numbered them - for example Taupo 1, 2 and 3. One area chosen was on a hillside where Mark's parents decided they would eventually build their house and Mum was keen to name it after a lake in Scotland as that is where her forbearers came from! But this small dam proved to have unsuitable clay content, having been chosen just for the view and actually never held the water that ran into it. However, the house site was never used anyway as the parents moved down to a second farm we developed later, down on the South coast at Cape Riche.

As I have said some areas were prone to salt degradation which produced evidence of scouring in the sheep and areas of land where no plants grew because the salt had risen from underneath the ground leaving it bare. We did not appreciate the extent of this salt problem and that it was better to leave the existing ti tree and natural bush covering the lower flat areas of the farm. We got the bulldozers to chain and then we burnt the creek bed of the River Perup. We thought we could open up the long narrow country to make it easier for the stock to get around to graze and easier for us to move them and so make efficient use of the area. That proved a mistake, as the original ti tree grew back as the land was too salty for anything else at that time.

In later years there were other salt tolerant grasses available to plant and these subsequently self-seeded. We planted clumps of a saltwater tolerant couch grass. This provided reasonable stockfeed to a small number of adult sheep whose gut was able to cope with the less palatable feed and also the access to salty water. It was not suitable for younger sheep as it tended to encourage worms in their intestines, plus the salty water was not good for them to drink as it made them scour. Over the years new grasses and clover have proved more salt tolerant and we gradually produced more palatable cover for the sheep to feed on in the gullies, which in turn helped to reduce the salt content and thus produced a very satisfactory area in which to run any age group of sheep. Eventually the salt content diminished to such an extent that the water also proved totally drinkable. Another learning curve for us.

Introduction To BUSHFIRES

A fire came in from the surrounding forestry land just after taking over the property in January whilst the previous owner was still living in the shack and before I had arrived in Australia. The little Ferguson tractor (Fergie as it was later named) made some fire breaks around the sheds by towing a big lump of old iron machinery to scrape up the dirt.

Local farmers always flocked to a fire with their water and pumps. They brought rakes and hessian bags to fight the flames, and tractors with blades to quickly create better fire breaks around the buildings.

I was told that Mum was kept very busy making loads of sandwiches and brewing copious mugs of tea for all the kind firefighters and the blaze was thankfully quelled in no time. The local response was magnificent and created an opportunity for many of the locals to see and meet the newbies – which they were all dying to do of course! It was also a chance for the newcomer Embrys to find out and enjoy the sampling of the local Swan Lager. This was always available at a fire scene once the mopping up work had been done and the fire scene was safe!

MARK AND I

Mark and I originally met at the age of fourteen, at Headquarters Fighter Command at Stanmore where his father was the Commander in Chief. My father was on the medical staff at the headquarters and our respective mothers arranged that we should have a game of tennis one day during the summer holidays. Apparently, Mark was not too impressed at playing a girl, but we were both pleasantly surprised as we were fairly evenly matched. This started a long platonic relationship. My brother, eighteen months older than me got frequent invitations with his young sister tagging along! We spent a summer of tennis, cricket and even rugby and as I was a tomboy it all suited me. If the weather was inclement, we retired inside and played table tennis, rummy, canasta and poker with matchsticks! Mark and I saw each other spasmodically after that but my father was then posted out to Germany and we did not renew our friendship until Mark was doing his National Service and was also posted to Germany, and it eventually became more than a platonic friendship! We got engaged in the romantic 'Foret de Fontainebleu' and when Mark emigrated to the Antipodes I followed after I had turned 21 - and the rest is history!

When living in Germany I had met some Australian sheep farmers on a cricket tour of some of the RAF stations in Germany. I surmised that sheep farming in Australia must be a wealthy occupation which was good news as I had just become engaged to Mark and we were going to join the family partnership in Australia to sheep farm. I concluded that all I would have to do was lean on a five-bar wooden gate, chewing on a straw, and watch the grass and wool grow! My reasoning being that wool had been a pound sterling for a pound in weight in recent years, so must be a lucrative occupation!

Mark had told me that the River Perup ran through the middle of the farm and so I thought we could eventually build a house overlooking this "river "and life would be wonderful! Mark always told me he had not lied. It was marked on the map as a river, but it was, in reality a muddy little creek that meandered its way through the local trees and ti tree bushes and dried up to form little pools of salty water in the summer!

This did in no way dampen my enthusiasm at the time, but it did sometimes make me pause to think at a later date!

I did not emigrate (as a £10 pom) until I had turned 21, arriving on the ship "New Australia" that went round the Cape of Good Hope as the Suez Canal was then closed. The journey took a whole month, and I was heartily glad to leave the ship on arrival at Fremantle where Mark met me when the ship docked. He drove me up to King's Park and showed me a few sights. Perth seemed to me to be a little provincial town after the size of some of the British cities I was accustomed to! The next day we drove down to the farm at Boyup Brook.

My first impressions were that lots of houses seemed to be single storey (bungalows - as we called them in England) and we passed through what seemed to me to be little villages on lots of empty roads with a few cars and trucks. There were a lot of green "fields" in pretty flat countryside with a range of green hills on our left. The Indian Ocean was apparently on our right, but not visible. Houses on farms were again mostly single storey but appeared picture book attractive, surrounded by green pastures, many with dairy cows grazing in the sunshine.

After 80 miles or so we headed left winding up through the hills. We very quickly entered green "bush" which seemed to be all a dull, dark green with a sameness in colour which seemed rather unattractive and boring after the ever- changing greens of verdant English pastures. We came across patches of farming countryside with sheep and cattle in the paddocks (as I learned to call them). A lot of the paddocks contained pushed over heaps of timber and rough, unkempt looking pastures and there seemed to be no houses, just small wooden sheds, with corrugated iron roofs – many of which I came to realise were small, temporary houses.

Eventually we came to what was our local town - Boyup Brook - where I was told our shops, schools and hospital were situated. The farm was another 30 miles onwards. Farms got less and less in number and there was more and more bush to drive through, and then the tarmac stopped and the road became dirt and gravel with farms hidden from view down bush tracks in amongst the timber and bushes! And as the light was fading, we eventually came to the farm.

Mark's eldest brother Keith was in a small lean- to shed "crutching" sheep in the failing light - all to be explained to me another day! Mark's parents arrived back to the farm having gone into town to get another Tilley lamp for the shack. "Buckingham Palace "as it was called, was the abode for us all for the next year or so. I was made to feel very welcome, and it was great to see Mark's parents again, although in rather different circumstances to the palatial Fontainebleau house in France!

The following days were all exciting and new as Mark took me around the farm in Keith's little Austin Ute and I saw his sheep dog Floss in action. I had great trouble seeing the sheep against the backdrop of the khaki-coloured pasture amid the ghostly grey dead trees, both standing and littering the ground. The Merino woolly sheep were greyish in colour and blended in with the landscape. Floss was a black and white Border Collie and Mark had bought her already trained to go round a mob of sheep and bring them back to him or drove them up a road or in the paddock. It was fascinating to watch her in action obeying Mark's commands on a whistle. A good sheep dog is worth more than three people and very necessary on the farm where there was so much debris on the ground in many of the paddocks.

I did make sure that Mark understood that I would not work to the whistle and come running at any time!

Over the years we had many sheepdogs on the farm, and some breeds were better for certain jobs. The Border Collie was basically a paddock dog and what was known as a good heading and droving dog. We also had the red kelpies that were good barking dogs and usually robust hustlers of the sheep for yard work. (They possibly were part derived from the dingo breed) Some could be trained to jump on the backs of the sheep in a race, in the sheep yards or in a sheep crate on a truck to move the sheep around. Even cattle got hustled with their barking and nipping the back of their hocks to encourage movement, and of course most of the dogs could jump around the yards. One dog of Mark's could single out a fly- blown sheep in a mob (when blowflies had concentrated on an area of skin under the wool and made that area rotten and smell by literally starting to eat the sheep alive). Once separated, the affected sheep could be run down with the motorbike thus enabling him to catch it and deal with it. Mark would either isolate the patch of fly blown wool, remove it with hand clippers and pour disinfectant around the area. If it was more affected he would bring the sheep in and shear it, and then very often had to shoot it as it was too badly fly struck.

Blowfly strike was a terrible curse to deal with and especially prevalent when there had been warm humid weather, when the sheep were at all soiled at their rear ends and when they were heavy in wool. - hence the preventative methods of crutching and dagging at certain times of the year. If a fly blown sheep was not located and treated the inevitable result was a horrible death as the maggots laid in the wool eventually ate into the flesh.

Buckingham Palace

This building did not look very impressive from the outside and appeared quite small to be housing six people. It was an incredible building of wood and odd bits of corrugated iron on four main tree trunks, with cardboard as much as wooden walls I thought! There was a lining of cardboard on three of the four walls which provided a rather gaudy wallpaper. We could read such colourful slogans as "Rinso – open and display now"; "H.M.V." "This way up" and many advertising wines. As the family said, "Anyone would think we boozed a lot!" The other walls were adorned with the previous owner's calendars - Winston Churchill alongside pretty popsies etc! Probably these all helped to hold the walls up and certainly kept the draughts out! All the walls had one narrow shelf lining them, so that bottles of tomato ketchup, chutney & jams, etc competed with the gaudy wallpaper! More cardboard lining was added to the walls by the new inmates and these advertised Orlando wines, Victoria bitter beers and a range of whiskeys and sherries!

When I arrived, I had my camp bed in one corner of the kitchen/living area. The big triangular shelf above my head was for my use, along with the bottles of booze (rather handy!) My square trunk was my bedside table/come clothes cupboard.

My wardrobe clothes shared the same hanging space as Mark's parents, which was my full-length plastic cover hanging in the doorway to their bedroom, next door to the kitchen. Their bedside tables were a packing case and a filing cabinet next to two single camp beds.

The boys' room had two camp beds in it and a hessian sack hanging halfway down in the doorway. So as can be imagined nowhere was soundproof! They had a door opening to the outside which had to be wedged tightly shut during inclement weather and to keep the cats out at any other time!

The bathroom beyond the boys' room was not soundproof either and was of corrugated iron construction with plenty of holes for ventilation! Quite a novel experience to see the moon through a hole in the roof when in the bath. The bath water was heated in the copper outside by burning wood (no shortage of that!) and so at least we got hot water although not quite on tap so to speak but bucketed into the tin bath. Nice hot water but bathing bordered on the "unpleasant" to "the distinctly unpleasant", depending on which quarter the wind was blowing from. However, we did kid ourselves that it became a "brick and tiled bathroom" as Dad built a brick and cement runaway drain for the bath water to exit after our ablutions were finished! Progress and comparative luxury!

The wash house or laundry was outside by the copper, so we had to don our waterproofs and scrub in the rain if it was a wet day. Then there was the dilemma of where to hang the wet clothes. Actually, apart from limited space in the shed recently vacated by the family (which proved almost open to the heavens anyway) there was only outside!

My 'mother-in-law- to -be' was an incredible woman. There was a wood-burning, antiquated kitchen range, rather badly designed, which dominated the kitchen and gave us warmth and cooking ability. There was also a temperamental Aladdin kerosene (paraffin) stove, but she managed to produce marvellous meals for us all. I still remember the huge tin of ginger snaps which came out when we had a cup of tea!

Hardly any of the floor in the shack was on the level and was covered with nondescript bits of linoleum which gradually lessened with every daily sweeping of the floor. The padding of cardboard and newspaper did tend to keep some of the draughts out. There was one small window at the back of this kitchen opening onto a big wooden shed. This window was usually left shut, as it opened onto some smelly sheep yards. The only door into the shack had to be kept open, if possible, as otherwise it was hard to see indoors, and during inclement weather we had to light the Tilley lamps to dispel the gloom indoors.

As can be imagined this cramped living heightened the need for more space in our living conditions. I am afraid the original idea was to put up a habitation quickly based on the plan that eventuated, but with different materials using fibro walls and a tin roof. This could have been quickly erected and available for habitation much earlier. But Dad's ideas were different, and bricks and mortar were his choice that he was intent on building with. Dad was on his building journey and left most of the farming and clearing to us, except at pressure periods. But this method of building did take longer than planned and was yet another example of his determination to live HIS dream.

However, that building took a back seat as the pressure was on to finish building the wool shed before our first shearing in October. Keith and Dad were basically involved with this as Mark was gaining experience and working for a nearby sheep farmer, and Paddy, the 14-year-old youngest son, was at boarding school in Perth.

The Workers

Dad managed to recruit some additional workers at the weekends. There was a sawmill, a flax mill and a narrow-gauge railway operating from Perth through Boyup Brook during our early years on the farm. Some Italian and Polish workers working in these areas were more than happy to be employed to help with the original clearing up of the paddocks at the weekends. Their motto was "picka the sticka quicka" and their help was invaluable in those early days, so it was well worth the effort of running them out to the farm and back to Boyup Brook.

The leader of the gang was one Polish worker called Jan who had escaped from Poland and Russia during the war and ended up working on the railway in Boyup Brook. He was the main organiser and boss of this motley workforce and became a tried and true friend over the years. He was forever indebted to Mark's father for helping him locate his mother in later years in Eastern Germany, behind the Iron Curtain. Yet another of the many examples of Dad's interest and support in providing assistance for many people he came in contact with during his Service and then civilian life, even out in Australia. Many of the "New Australians," as they were known as in those days, were from Italy, (but most of them had fought on the Russian front – or so they said!) and came from Poland and Germany and Dad got on with them all extremely well.

This international band of workers turned their hand to any sort of a job - digging holes for sleepers for the sheep and cattle yards; mixing concrete and helping with the erection of the metal trusses for the new wool shed being built. A fairly hairy job I came to realise as we had not got a tractor equipped with front hydraulics to run a loader and blade for lifting. So, it was all done with ropes and brute strength! How no one had a truss drop on their head still amazes me! Fairly dicey work! But most of their work in between these specialised jobs, was clearing and burning timber for quite a few years!

First Jobs

After the weekend Mark went off to his job with an excellent sheep farmer in the district, who farmed about 10 miles down the road. He was learning basically about sheep and wool. The wool from Merino sheep is a different fibre to the crossbred sheep he had worked with in New Zealand. They were more of a meat animal, not bred for the woollen trade. This was all new to him, as it was to all of us except for his brother Keith who had been farming for quite some time in Rhodesia and New Zealand. Mark learnt a lot and was then able to class the wool clip at shearing time which meant we did not have to employ a wool classer which would have been quite expensive. Basically, different parts of a sheep's body grow wool of different lengths and quality, which is separated at shearing time. For example, the belly wool is shorter and can be discoloured and needs to go in a separate line to the fleece wool off the main body of the sheep. The main body wool is longer in staple, softer to handle and more attractive in colour and crimp. It is a major part of the fleece and is the most valuable.

Dad and Keith were basically flat out building the three-stand shearing shed and so I was very quickly taught to drive the little Ferguson tractor with a posthole digger mounted on the hydraulics on the back. I followed one of our neighbouring farmers who walked ahead of me marking the holes to be dug for the Jarrah telephone poles that were going to be put in by us local landowners. A party telephone line was going to bring the 20th century communication to us and neighbouring farmers, after we had attached the insulators and wires. No mobile phones in those days! The "party line" was operated by the wife of the local forestry manager living about ten miles from us. Conversations were not sacred to privacy as the operator could theoretically be aware of what was said. However, she proved a very efficient and helpful secretary at times, informing the caller that the best time to contact us was in the evenings when they would be sure to find us at home out of the paddocks! She also was adept at taking messages to pass on to us! Certainly, it was vastly better than not having a phone at all, and this continued for several years.

A Fordson Dexta tractor was purchased which had more engine power and heavier hydraulics, and I was then put to use disk ploughing fire breaks around the ring barked and bush perimeters of the farm. That job proved invaluable in helping me to find my way around some of the farm.

My driving capabilities were also used for running the 30 miles into Boyup Brook to get welding done on various bits of the shearing shed etc, after I had received some instructions on how to drive on dirt roads.

Driving on the dirt roads in Australia took a bit of getting used to, as we had to drive virtually in the middle-of-the-road to avoid most of the ruts and potholes. It was possible to see someone coming as they were accompanied by a cloud of dust! When we did meet someone, we had to move over of course and be ready for the cloud of dust and some reduced visibility after passing alongside each other. A different story in the winter when it was possible to see quite a long way ahead because the dust was dampened down.

The main roads in WA are mostly very good compared with other States and many of them are bituminised. But dirt roads need to be graded to maintain a reasonable surface and of course this does not happen on such a regular basis in country areas. I also found that it was necessary to keep up a good speed on dirt roads to ride the ruts and potholes better.

There was a 30-inch average annual winter rainfall for the farm and to me it must have all fallen in that month of June after my arrival! Where was this sunny Australia I had seen on all the posters back in the UK?! The dampness seemed to be accentuated by the almost dreary looking dank dark green of the native bush, but it did not seem cold and did not last. Once July came the rain was intermittent, there was lots of sunshine and so we were mostly in shirtsleeves.

Fencing proved to be another major occupation for Keith and myself, plus Mark when he was home on the weekends. We concentrated on fencing the boundaries to start with, using high wooden posts supplied from local timber mills scattered throughout the surrounding bush. We assembled the fence with wire and rabbit netting dug into the ground to keep rabbits out and with a high wire to discourage jumping kangaroos! Once the shearing shed was basically assembled Dad was left to install the tongued and grooved wooden flooring and the grating for the sheep holding pens whilst we concentrated on constructing the sheep yards around the shed. Of course, we had the help from the international band of weekend workers from Boyup Brook which speeded up things a lot.

I took to this work very quickly and absolutely loved being out in the fresh air and learning new things every day. I just about became welded to the seat of that tractor as I loved using the blade to push together fires and burning up logs, and there was plenty of that over the years!

Not many people are able to enjoy such freedom of spirit that involves the senses as well as their occupation in life and this is how it seemed to me in my new life at "Ardua". I had always preferred digging in the garden to trying to bake cakes in the kitchen! I was always an out of doors person and this new lifestyle seemed ideal to me. I enjoyed the outdoor work that I was doing and the new responsibilities that I was challenged with.

Shearing Shed

Once Dad had completed the tongued and grooved flooring in the woolshed Mark's parents put their double bed up in the shed and moved out of the shack. At least they had the comfort of a proper bed, but they did have to use covers to protect the bedding from the damp drips from the cold corrugated iron roof above them every morning in the winter! They also had to share the bed with the sheep when we had a mob penned up for crutching or shearing. The sheep were on the grating floor in the shed annexe and so their dung and urine dropped underneath through the slats but of course there was a very pungent smell and the noise of their urinating, combined with the odour of the lanolin in the wool probably took a bit of getting used to! Sheep are also very restless creatures moving around, scraping their hooves, coughing and urinating and are therefore quite noisy under those conditions.

So, the soft bed wasn't all it promised to be!

The flooring also continued on to the "shearing board" where three shearing stands had been erected to run the overhead gear to operate the cutting handpieces. An annexe with grating floor and catching pens was then assembled to hold the sheep before shearing them. Meanwhile we were outside building the wooden sheep yards and ramp up into the annexe for the sheep to enter the pens. The flooring of the whole shed was raised well off the ground so that we could store sheep to be shorn underneath the tongued and grooved section of flooring if the weather was threatening rain.

A small engine room was built at ground level joining onto the shed with a concrete floor and a cement block for one of the two Lister diesel engines Dad had brought out in a packing case from the UK. This engine ran the overhead shearing gear that operated the handpieces that the shearers used. These handpieces were quite heavy and got quite warm as the combs and cutters cut their way through the fleece on the sheep, pressed down against the skin on the body of the sheep.

So, we were then ready to shear our first mob of sheep, our 400 wethers, which took two shearers three days using two of the three stands we had built. It was fascinating to watch a shearer in action. Like all experts they made it look easy to our untrained eyes and expert shearers can turn out 200 sheep a day or more. However, they took it easy for us as we were just learning on the job! We learnt how to deal with the fleece wool and the wool pieces and produced our first few bales of wool for sale with the "Ardua" stencil marked on the outside of the hessian wool bales! It was a very proud moment when these stencilled bales left on a truck bound for the wool sale in Fremantle.

The name" Ardua" was given to the farm by Mum and Dad. It was chosen from the RAF motto "Per Ardua ad Astra" (By hard work to the stars) and we thought it proved very apt. Indeed, we used to call it "Arduous Ardua" at times!

The Cottage

Atruckload of building materials had arrived on the farm before I had arrived, and Dad had started the building. The first house was built with red bricks (more or less with book in one hand and trowel in the other). The idea was to build to a very basic design which would become shearers' quarters afterwards. There was a reasonably sized kitchen/living room, two bedrooms and a bathroom/shower. The rooms opened onto a long veranda facing up one of the valleys. Lovely breezes used to waft up to the inmates as they sat and had their evening drinks, after a hot day's work. Once the footings were in, the brick walls grew fairly rapidly. Wooden floor bearers, roof trusses and wooden window frames with louvre windows were installed. The roof tiles were made of concrete which meant the roof trusses had to be quite robust to take the weight. The wooden trusses were assembled on the ground. There were more aerial acrobatics by the boys to lift the trusses and place them up on the walls. Working with Jarrah timber entailed first drilling holes for the nails as it is an extremely hard wood and a heavy lift.

We had to work out a running water solution for the cottage. We built a metal tank stand and hauled a 4000-gallon galvanised corrugated metal tank with a rope round the tank. We pulled it up by tractor from the back of a truck, balanced on two long pieces of piping from the decking of the truck up to the tank stand. A fairly hairy operation but it worked. The rain-water was collected from the roof off the gutters and then grav-ity fed into the house for use in the kitchen, shower and toilet. The cottage, as we called it, was finished after about eighteen months and the boys moved up to their bedroom. I was left in solitary splendour in Buckingham Palace, but able to use the facilities in the cottage. What bliss to have a hot shower and toilet facilities, even if I had to walk a hundred metres or so. I was to remain in the shack until Mark and I were married.

A 240-volt generator was installed in the engine room of the shed to provide lighting for the cottage. This was a great boon for us all as we said farewell to the Tilley lamps, except in an emergency. We had to crank up the Lister to start it every night and later walk over to the woolshed to turn it off when we retired to sleep. It was magic for us all and Mum and Dad were no longer sleeping in the woolshed. The engine noise might have been too much for them to ignore!

The concrete tiles left over from the house were eventually used for a chook house (henhouse). Dad built a very fine one out of wood, with clinker built slabbing wooden walls and a big window (covered with rabbit netting) for ventilation, plus a tiled roof. It must have been the finest chook house in WA, if not in the whole of Australia. So nice and cool for the hens in the hot weather.

Forestry Department

In the depression years owners had to walk off their small blocks as the farms were then, which meant that the land titles reverted to the Crown. This meant we could knock over timber and use it for fence strainers (anchor points for the wire between fence posts), or actual posts, or we could burn it up - but we could not sell it. We weep for all that beautiful timber that just went up in smoke. Jarrah is such a beautiful, deep red hardwood, highly sought after in the furniture trade through the centuries and a great sturdy and strong timber for roofs of houses etc. The sale of it would have really helped us tremendously in the cost of clearing the farm over the years.

We were about to clear the first big block of virgin bush (approximately 300 acres) when the Forestry Department decided they wanted to gain access. They wanted to cut the big trees down, leaving the many large stumps in the ground, cutting off the canopies and carting the logs away to be sold. Dad said he wanted them to bulldoze these big Jarrah trees, stump and all. We were not interested in having them cut down (thus leaving us with the stumps). It would then have cost us twice as much again to dig the stumps out with the bulldozer.

Our suggestion was that the trees should be knocked over by the bulldozer, and that the dozer would leave the Forestry logs out, separate to the windrows. Then the Forestry could come in and cut the stumps and canopies off, taking the logs away on their jinkers (trailers). This operation would cost *us* a bit more as the bulldozer then had to push the remnants and stumps into the heaps to burn in a separate operation, but less than the way they wanted to do it. They were not too enamoured with this proposal, but he told them in no uncertain terms (as was his wont over his many years in the Royal Air Force) that his way was the only way, and he would make it as difficult as possible for them to get into the logs and then truck them out on their jinkers. The jut of his jaw and his piercing blue eyes very soon convinced the powers- that- be that he meant business and his service record went before him, and so they very wisely acceded to his plan.

This solution was reminiscent of his negotiation skills during the war! When he was CO at RAF Wittering, he had the brainwave to extend the existing runway, clearing a small coppice of light timber and bushes, to connect with a small unused aero club facility. The extension would greatly aid the return landing of bombers, especially if they were in a shot-up state and limping back after night operations. He approached the landowner who agreed and indeed assisted with his heavy machinery to clear and level the area. Armed with a bottle of whisky Dad then approached another farmer who had put in a crop of potatoes on the aero club site and offered to buy the crop, in the ground, so that the area could be released to extend the flare path. He approached the Works & Bricks outfit (at Air Ministry) to authorise and install a flare path for the runway. That request gained a negative reply, as concern was raised that it might be an amateurish job and some of their people could get electrocuted.

Dad's reply was "How many people do you think will be electrocuted? because I am prepared to endanger four or five of them to save one bomber load of highly skilled aircrew. There is a war on!"

The runway was extended, and many aeroplanes limped in in their shot-up states and from many other squadrons too over the years.

Basically Dad got on well with people over the years. He was a real charmer with his blue eyes and sense of humour, but also that backbone of steel and unerring application to whatever job was on hand. This usually convinced people that he was not one to be trifled with or argued against. He did not suffer fools gladly and red tape was anathema to him, as it had been throughout his service career. If someone had said "No" he would ask who had told him "No". He would then progress up the chain of command to the person in charge, who invariably turned out to be amenable to discussion, or had never said" No", in the first place! Sounds like the government and businesses of yesteryear and today!

Sheep

Initially we bought in fully grown Merino wethers (neutered male sheep) for wool production. These sheep could cope with the basic pasture that grew amongst the ring barked timber of the semi-cleared paddocks.

We began to improve the native grasses by applying fertilisers and clover seeds. This allowed us to purchase some Merino ewes and mate them to Merino rams, keeping the bulk of the ewe lambs as breeding sheep for ongoing wool income. The wether lambs we kept for wool growing income, and they eventually ended up on the live sheep ship, traded to the Middle East.

We also grew lupin crops on the new areas we cleared. We bought in some Border Leicester rams to put to Merino ewes and produced a separate flock of crossbred lambs for the fat lamb market. Any lambs that did not make the grade were kept for six months, or so, then sold as hoggets for the local meat trade.

We gradually built up these different flocks of sheep, increasing in numbers, and increasing our income each year.

Calendar

Time and years passed really quickly on the farm. We lived and worked so much through the different seasons within the year. The seasons appeared topsy-turvy to me since the hottest weather in WA was in December and January. It took a while to adjust to a hot Christmas day! The summer months across the other side of the world were actually winter months in WA. Over the years we have tended to have a hot Christmas meal on Christmas Eve and then fish, cold meats and salad on Christmas Day. In the early days we really felt the heat of the summer around the middle of the day. In January and February, we would often get up early at 5am and put in a couple of hours of stick picking before breakfast. We were picking up sticks and throwing them into the bulldozed heaps or creating smaller heaps to be burnt when the burning season was declared 'open' at the end of February. We would continue working until midday out in the paddocks. After lunch we would do stuff at home and around the sheds, until the main heat had gone at around 4pm.

Our annual calendar roughly followed this program for many of the early years:

January: (in the heat of summer) we kept the suction clover harvester going; the ever-present occupation of stick picking and preparing the paddocks for burning up with the bulldozer.

End of February: the bulldozer/s in, burning season opened. We lit up the bulldozed heaps, burning large and small heaps with the proper fire breaks around. We also had an army of neighbours with their fire trucks and tractors on hand on the day we initially lit up, to make the whole operation safely monitored. Then stick picking, burning and finally levelling the cleared land with discing and harrowing. There would be a slight blue haze and pall of gum smoke around the farming areas at that time, as everyone in the district was involved as we were. I used to love that time even though it was hard work.

March/April: hopefully the break of the season with rain! Fertilising and seeding crops. Supplementary feeding with grain to sheep (mostly oats and lupins) extending into May/June depending on the feed situation in the paddocks.

May/June: animal husbandry. Lambing ewes and needling all sheep for protection against pulpy kidney disease. Crutching all sheep (this operation involved pulling the sheep across the board in the wool shed to shear some wool off the sheep's bottom and inside of the crutch to inhibit soiling of the wool in that area). Ideally this kept the individual sheep clean for the shearing operation later in the year.

July/August: lambing, lamb marking, drenches, needling. Maintenance jobs and fencing.

September: dagging dirty sheep i.e., cleaning up any dags on the crutches of sheep in preparation for shearing.

October: shearing the main flock of sheep and dipping to protect them against lice. Dipping was superseded after a few years with 'back lining' individual sheep in a race, with a liquid preparation against lice (this proved much quicker and easier on both the animal and the operator!)

November/December: shearing and selling of lambs and the start of harvesting grain, such as oats, lupins and vetches.

Any spare time during these months meant the interminable job of stick picking in preparation for lighting up and burning when the season opened.

This was the basic program through the years, whilst we were clearing and developing and everyone around us was in the same boat, so to speak! Farming conversations were basically around how much clearing we were doing; when the opening rains would come; comparing notes on how much rain we got on individual farms; the prices of stock at the local markets and the price they got on the auction floor for their wool.

It was such a great occupation to be involved in because I found the conversation with the male farmers so much more interesting than discussing cake recipes etc., and I seemed to be accepted more as an equal because of what I was doing. Not that there weren't many wives of farmers involved in the daily running of the farm, but there seemed to be a separation of the sexes when it came to discussing the daily events of farming. This was evident at social gatherings, where the men would congregate at one end of the room and discuss interesting things and events on the farm and the ladies would be at the other end, discussing cake recipes and babies! Or so it seemed to me!

Another amusing fact about farmers probably the world over is that the luck of the Gods is either with them or against them weatherwise! Very often the farmer on one side of the fence wants fine weather because he is shearing but his neighbour wants rain for his crops!

Weather almost invariably occupies the conversation whenever two or more farmers meet, but it causes great amusement for the onlookers. The saying goes "once a farmer

always a farmer" and so in retirement we are quite often con-
scious of the hot humid weather that can encourage fly strike
in the unshorn sheep, or rain in the middle of summer that
can wreck a crop before harvest by badly staining the grain,
consequently reducing its value to the grower.

Cranbrook Road

The Cranbrook Road was a gravel road which ran roughly through the middle of our farm. Originally surveyed as a railway, it was a very handy all-weather track and stock race for moving sheep around our farm. But it was also the main road from Boyup Brook to other outlying farms. The mail truck from Boyup Brook could come through and deliver mail and stores, such as food and farming essentials, for us and the other farms three days a week. For some reason the cost of the run was subsidised in lieu of the railway that never got built. Thank goodness not - a railway could have proved a real fire hazard for us. Other trucks and vehicles came through the middle of the farm, using this road, which proved a nuisance when we were moving mobs of sheep. We had to have someone ahead warning any oncoming traffic. Big trucks, with jinkers loaded with huge logs, also came through periodically.

Once when we were moving a mob of sheep, a log truck came up behind us with the driver gesticulating madly for Mum to get out of the way. Obviously, his brakes were not what they should have been! Fortunately, he did manage to stop before the sheep -just - but we had to leap aside. We did suggest to Mum that she should have let the truck run over her foot as we could have done a lot of clearing on the compensation cheque!

Frugal Beginnings

Those were desperate years starting out on Ardua. We had to get land cleared and productive to start to gain an income. We were living pretty frugally; in that we did not have a lot of money to spend on our personal requirements. Mum's veggie garden provided beautiful fresh vegetables for us all. Our meat was plentiful, as we produced it ourselves. We made sure we killed our crossbred sheep for the table, not the old tough Merinos that a lot of Australian farmers butchered and naturally the boys had to learn to butcher the sheep for the table. We milked a cow which gave us plentiful milk and cream. Our grocery bills were kept to the minimum, as we were so self-contained, and all things considered we thought that we lived pretty well.

The odd trip to Perth kept up the wine supply. Many of the vineyards, in the Swan Valley in Perth, sold sherry by the gallon if we took an empty flagon along! We couldn't afford beer but sherry was very acceptable. These were the days before wine was plentiful and cheap at the vineyards!

A very good friend of the family was a spinster lady in her 80s, known as Dilly, who lived in Perth and was a great friend of many RAF people. During the war she had been a pilot in the air transport auxiliary, ferrying aircraft to squadrons and bases throughout the British Isles and returning aircraft from airfields across the channel. These female pilots often flew without radio or navigation aids and in the foulest of weather when operational flying was on hold, to keep the planes in the air, wherever they were needed.

Dilly had an old green Singer motorcar and used to don big leather gauntlets when at the wheel. A fascinating lady, she seemed to know so many illustrious and titled people throughout the world and had many a tale to tell. She had once had a tyre changed at the top of the Simplon Pass in France by a man, who later became Pope John! Dilly was always very generous to the Embry family, giving any of us beds when we went to Perth, and we always had a base when we spent the odd day and night up there.

Our many friends in Perth were so generous with their offers of showers and baths when we arrived to stay with them - not because we were "on the nose" (or I don't think so!) They knew of our living conditions and that it was such a treat to have unlimited hot water cascading out of taps!

Basic living and basic clothing with new items mostly work-related (such as work boots and work clothing) and living out in the bush made life very simple but fulfilling, I would not have changed it for anything!

Alas, it did mean that Mark and I did not have much independence from the rest of the family, as regards transport. There were only the two vehicles – Dad's A70 Austin shooting brake and Keith's small Austin Ute. They were very generous in allowing us to borrow one or the other to go to cricket, or travel to Perth for a break – but it meant we always had to ask, and they always knew where we were going! Sounds silly – but we did find it rather irksome to not have that modicum of independence!

Financial Challenges

I guess Dad's dream had been slightly tarnished by the heavy clearing costs that were mounting up. The liquidity problems had been further accentuated by a couple of unforeseen and devastating financial challenges, plus the increasing Bank interest rates.

The first challenge was not of a huge financial cost but would have left an unpleasant taste in his mouth. Dad joined the very new Royal Air Force, as opposed to the RFC (Royal Flying Corp), at the age of 18 and was awarded a short service commission. His choice of career was not approved of by his father - the Anglican vicar of Dover - because it was the "Junior Service", very new and untried! He cut his teeth, so to speak, on biplanes such as the Tiger Moth and Vickers Vernon. In Afghanistan he flew over the mountainous terrain, desert sand plains and wadis, as the British basically controlled the warring tribesmen from the air.

When Dad received his permanent commission at the age of 21, he was told he had a choice. He could take the gratuity awarded to him straight away at the end of his short service commission or put it towards his eventual pension at the end of his service career in the RAF. He elected to leave his gratuity in situ. However, at the end of his career he was informed that since he had elected not to receive that sum of money earlier it was no longer available! In other words they had changed the goalposts.

The second challenge he faced was to do with the autobiography Mission Completed. He had signed up to lucrative instalment rights of this book with a UK newspaper. However, before he left for New Zealand he had had a good chat with a senior retired RAF officer about the content of the book. This officer expressed reservations at one of the chapters and a concern that the content could prove damaging to the Royal Air Force. Dad's whole life and commitment had been, and still was, to the RAF. He certainly never wanted to harm its image in any way and so he removed this one chapter from publication.

This caused the newspaper to remove their very lucrative offer, which would have been of great financial assistance.

The final challenge was again over his autobiography. He started writing it after leaving the RAF whilst staying in France. He wrote it on board his sea trip to New Zealand, continued writing it and finished it after getting to New Zealand. Not one word of it was written in the UK. But – he was resident in New Zealand for less than an obligatory six months.

So the proceeds of the book, added to his final year of income, placed him in one of the highest tax brackets. The British taxation authorities then claimed the taxation rights on the book, which pushed his taxable income as an Air Chief Marshal into the super tax bracket. He took counsel from a friend, who was an eminent QC, who said "Basil you have a good case, but you will not win, and all you can do is come to some agreement with the Treasury".

So, he agreed to relinquish his wartime gratuities as settlement. It is hard to imagine that someone who had lived his life risking it for his country during wartime should have to relinquish the monetary reward awarded by that country, on a technicality!

Cars

Dad bought an Austin A70 station wagon whilst in France before his Fontainebleau appointment at Allied Air Forces Central Europe was completed. Transported to New Zealand, and then back to WA, it proved a stalwart vehicle for the start of the Ardua project. The Austin had a very reliable engine but had not been made for Australian conditions, as the bodywork of the station wagon was of timber. Dad had not realized, or catered for, a dust proof vehicle such as were sold in Australia at that time. The Austin acted like a vacuum cleaner for the dust on gravel roads! We arrived at our destinations covered in fine red dust. When we got married and started our family the current baby in the basket in the back (before the days of baby capsules) was covered in fine red dust! However, the A70 did sterling work for all of us for quite a few years.

Dad still drove with the double de-clutch mentality, revving up the engine as he changed down gears, and his fame spread near and far with the locals. They all said "there goes Basil to church "as they heard the roar of the engine as he changed down to third gear, before taking the right-angled bend on the way to church in Boyup Brook early on a Sunday morning!

The only other mode of transport was Keith's little A40 ute which was brought over from New Zealand and performed well for years as well. A farm utility, or ute as they are commonly known as, consisted of a cab with a tray behind it which carried all sorts of things, especially on a farm. Both these vehicles had front bench seats and steering wheel gear sticks so they could carry three of us in front before the days of seat belts! This meant that Keith, Mark and I could squeeze into the ute and explore the South-west on day trips occasionally.

Welcomed

The Embry family were very warmly welcomed into the district and people were very supportive and helpful as we started our farming venture. Keith had been to agricultural College in England before he went overseas, but most of his farming was done in New Zealand. Mark went to work for a local farmer down the road and was learning the basics about sheep husbandry. Dad had dipped into many books, but mostly about farming in the UK. The locals passed on local knowledge about the seasons and the farming environment and were always very helpful in answering questions and giving basic advice. Of course, two eligible bachelors moving into the area created quite a stir too! When I turned up, six months later, there were many hopes dashed!

We had to get used to the terminology and customs of Australian country life. When we were invited to "come to tea" it meant the evening meal (dinner), not afternoon tea. "Bring a plate" meant bring something on it, such as sandwiches, cake, or biscuits. It was also the local custom to bring some bottles or cans of beer, or a bottle of wine. A very sensible custom which made every visit very pleasant and no great stress or expense for the host.

Another area we had to become familiar with was the local pub and the segregation of the ladies from the men! Mark's parents called into the local pub with two visiting friends and into the lounge for a beer. There was a group of ladies there, but no men.

"What's the matter with the men of Boyup Brook that they leave these lovely ladies all on their own?" queried Dad in a loud voice, not realising that the public bars were taboo to the fairer sex! He certainly made himself very popular with these ladies with his charm and humour.

Perhaps that was the catalyst for the change in drinking laws and more lenient regulations later in WA?!

Mark, and Paddy when he was at home from boarding school in Perth, were both enthusiastically welcomed into the local cricket team. The Mayanup Cricket Club was established 28 miles down the road from Boyup Brook, our nearest town. A little store and petrol pump were established in the middle of surrounding farmland and bush. Mark took great delight in letting our friends in the UK know that he had played for the MCC! The cricket was played on an oval that was dry khaki coloured grass and the batting strip was matting on top of a concrete base. There were five teams in the district at that time. We often had to travel some 30 miles in various directions to play cricket on similar wickets in what seemed to be in the middle of nowhere! This was our one release off the farm in the summer. It was greatly looked forward to every week. A welcome change of scene and time spent with other people, and for me a chance to mix with other women. We also occasionally played tennis at the local hard courts (concrete or bitumen) some 11 miles down the road in the opposite direction.

Apart from these outings it was work every day, week in/ week out, but all for a good cause!

Characters

The whole farming area seemed to contain many local identities who were such characters. We enjoyed meeting many of them, especially over those early years of clearing the bush on Ardua.

Dad was working on his first house, "the shearers quarters" - when a car drew up and out got two men. A very big man with rolled up sleeves and dirty torn trousers introduced himself as Monsignor Cunningham. Dad turned to the second occupant of the car and said – "Oh and I suppose you are the Bishop of Bunbury!" He wasn't but Dad was not used to the casual understatement of visitors in the bush, dressed for labour, especially a member of the clergy! Mons (as he informed us he was known as) was looking for somewhere to leave his bees to sample the Jarrah and White gum blossom, to make some honey. He left them for quite some time and Mum was very keen to help him when he came to get the honey. But we all gave the operation a wide berth - but greatly enjoyed the honey!

Mons had been a priest in the Australian Army in New Guinea during the war, so again Dad explored that theatre of war. They swapped many a story and became great friends. Mons also gave Dad some bricklaying advice as he had built quite a few church buildings in his time and was always a practical man.

Another great identity was Archie, an 80-year-old farmer on the neighbouring farm through the bush. He and his 75 year old wife had cleared their farm over the years and he greatly enjoyed yarns with Dad. He confessed that his only child, a daughter, had married this German lad who worked for the Forestry Department and Archie was not happy that she had brought a "Hun" into the family! He had virtually disowned them both and certainly was not going to leave the farm to his daughter. Dad persuaded him that by doing this he was not only depriving himself of his daughter, but that in fact "the Hun" was winning! At last, he reconciled himself to admitting them back to the fold.

Archie persuaded his bank manager to release the funds for the purchase of a small bulldozer. ("Just for fun" he said, as his eyes lit up). He then insisted on bringing it over and stacking up a lot of our ring- barked timber so that we could burn it. That proved invaluable in making the running of the wethers easier in semi-cleared paddocks that had had some sort of pasture sown in them over the years.

One evening Archie and his wife brought round a long lost 86 year old friend of theirs to meet Dad. We all spent a fascinating evening listening to the two old-timers sharing stories of their early days of clearing the land with oxen, horses and using crosscut saws and axes. They built their "humpies" to live in and travelled the bush with horse and cart to the local store 30 miles away to get their victuals. They spent the night on the road each way and returned with the basics for living for the next six months. It made us realise how easy we were getting it!

Another real old timer age 90 or so was Dave. He had the appearance of the proverbial biblical prophet with a long white beard and long white hair. He lived on his own in a little wooden house on a small property with long dry grass and sagging fences, running a few hundred Merino sheep. The local story was that he kept the holes in the sheep netting so that the sheep could get back in again to waterholes after fossicking for food in the bush.

Another story was that two young keen Taxation Department officials called in one day to audit his books as his taxation returns were non-existent. He ushered them into his kitchen where the old wood-burning Metters stove was alight to warm the room. He had a long tree trunk poked into its small firebox and occupying half the kitchen floor and as the wood burnt down Dave would push it in, saving a lot of time and effort with the axe! The result created both warmth and smoke in the room. The two taxation accountants withstood the smoke for so long but eventually gave up their inspection and with eyes streaming and lungs full of smoke gave a very basic assessment and then thankfully left!

Dave's eyes gleamed as he rubbed his hands together in glee as his taxation check was far less than he'd reckoned on it being!

First Crop

The first crop that we sowed at Ardua was oats to be harvested and kept for feeding the sheep at the break of season when feed was short in the paddocks. In those early days we took the crop off with a tractor drawn harvester and didn't have the luxury of handling the grain in bulk. In later years we had bulk storage harvesting bins, augers and silos. This grain was stored on our woolshed floor, in hessian bags, which we sewed shut with needle and string.

Very early on we discovered the Aussies called "a spade a spade" and were very direct and succinct in their speech, very often delivered with straight-faced humour!

Our next-door neighbour got us to take his crop off on contract and this was when my parents had come over to see us. My Dad walked across paddocks and through some bush to see the operation we were involved in and found us all sitting next to the header(harvester) having morning smokoe. He was invited to join us so sat down with his cup of tea and on seeing a plate of sandwiches said, "Shall I help myself?" The reply from the teenage son of our farmer neighbour was: "If you don't, no other......... will!" - much to my father's amusement. He said to us later: "Oh I bought that one didn't I?!"

Clover Rolling (Alec)

Alec was a very successful farmer in the district and lived about 10 miles down the road from us. He had cleared his farm in the clover rolling boom in the early days. He burnt the paddock and then scratched it up with harrows to bring the seed up on top. His method of obtaining the seed was to pull big rollers covered with wool sheepskins which gathered up the clover burrs containing the seed, which was then automatically scraped off into a bulk bin and was then bagged off into hessian bags. He ran a lot of fine wool Merino sheep and some black Aberdeen Angus cattle and so was extremely helpful with his advice and support.

He had been in the Australian Army serving in New Guinea during the war and Dad enjoyed swapping stories on their different theatres of war.

Alec had also been a shearer in his early farming days - so no one could "pull the wool over Alec's eyes" so to speak! One story goes that he drove to Perth to pick up his shearing team. As you can imagine shearing is constant heavy work and cold beers are always enjoyed after the day's work has finished. Shearers and shed staff greatly enjoyed a drink or three! The shearing team he had picked up accused him of not being a shearer way back before he bought his farm, because he had just driven past a pub on the outskirts of Perth! The challenge was made! They stopped at every pub they came to on the 180-mile trip back to Boyup Brook and it took three days! The story goes it took three weeks of shearing for the team to pay off their drinking debt to the boss!

As Alec had been so successful in the early days of developing his farm, using a clover rolling technique on the virgin country, and as we were clearing so much undeveloped country from scratch, we then decided it would be worth seeding each new area with a different type of clover. As it was virgin land there was no competition from pasture seeds. With the benefit of his knowledge and experience we purchased a clover harvesting machine which operated from the power take-off of the big second-hand Chamberlain tractor we bought. This proved a very good investment, and we made a lot of money off the sale of many different clovers which then paid for the clearing of the many acres of green bush on "Ardua" over the years.

Clover Harvesting

As the virgin bush was bulldozed, we cleared, levelled and seeded the land with different varieties of clover seed. As these crops were very pure, we could harvest them and sell the seed to other farmers who were also establishing their farmland from virgin bush. The green clover varieties we could grow, dried off in the summer and the tiny round hard clover seeds were contained in a small burr. Thousands of them lying on the ground. This dry vegetation was burnt off with a light controlled burn at the end of the day, with fire breaks around the area of course, and then next day worked up with small tractors pulling harrows behind them at a rate of knots. The harrows were a series of short spikes that crushed and broke up the burnt area and worked the small burrs up to the surface so they could be harvested. As you can imagine this was a very dusty job and appeared almost maniacal with no obvious reason for that operation when viewed by an onlooker! We all looked pretty disreputable covered in dust and grime and the water bag hanging in front of the radiators on the tractors took a fair bit of punishment in those times as it was thirsty work, but the seed threshed better in the heat of the day.

We then had to do a final pick-up of sticks and stones, walking over the harrowed area before the clover harvester went in to suck up the burr. This operation meant peoplepower of course, but we would cover the area pretty quickly dragging hessian bags for the small debris which we then dumped on piles of rocks in the paddock.

We purchased a state-of-the-art clover harvester which was a big noisy yellow tractor- drawn monster that sucked up the clover burrs off the ground and then thrashed the small clover seed out of the husks into rotating drums to end up in a storage bin for us to then bag off for sale. These bags proved very heavy due to the amount and the density of the seed in each bag. They were stored in the wool shed - the general-purpose storage shed for everything! This machine operated with a loud hum. It had what looked like a big chimney from which a large black cloud of dust and debris was exhaled as it went along. Dad used to drive the clover machine and it was probably the nearest he could get to a noisy Blenheim bomber! It was always easy to know where he was in the paddock with this dark column of dust going four feet upwards accompanied by the very loud humming noise, further giving away his position. A very grimy, dust covered Air Chief Marshal, with blue eyes, would flash his teeth in a smile as he dismounted to greet any visitor who gingerly offered his clean hand for a grubby handshake.

One day fortunately Mark was harrowing the clover fairly close to where Dad was working. Dad had got off his tractor to adjust something on the clover machine and had not applied the brake correctly. The whole outfit started to roll down a slight hill towards a dam full of water and Dad was trying to mount the tractor in front of the rear wheel, which was fraught with danger! Mark tore across the paddock on his little tractor shouting to him to jump clear and drew alongside, with the huge rear wheel of the big tractor towering above him. He then kept nudging it with his infinitely smaller rear wheel gradually knocking the big tractor off course until he slowly brought the whole outfit round the contour to a halt. Of course, there was no insurance cover for that sort of accident to the tractor or clover machine or the driver!

As we brought in many acres of virgin land every year we were able to grow many different varieties of clover seed - Woogenellup, Yarloop and Geraldton to name but a few. Some of these clovers were immortalised by our naming the paddocks they were sown in after these varieties. So many land-owners were clearing in these times that the demand for clover seed was very high and proved a lucrative aid to our clearing costs. The sheep in Australia are remarkable creatures. They eat green clover, as do sheep in all countries where it is grown, but the clover in the summer, which is that green feed in the paddock that has dried off, seems very palatable to them. Merino sheep in particular do extremely well on what appears to be a dry paddock with nothing edible there! They fossick for the small dry clover seeds as well as eating the roughage of the plants. The drier the ground appears and the more the feed appears to be non-existent - the finer the merino wool is grown on the sheep's back. Rain in the summer is not welcome as it can wreck this "dry feed".

Mayanup Fire

The Ardua farm was 30 miles out of Boyup Brook, 10 miles on bitumen and 20 miles on a dirt road (a gravel road with ruts and potholes). It was a hot, hot day when you felt as if you kicked your foot on a stone it could spark a fire.

Mark was playing cricket for his local team the M.C.C. (the Mayanup Cricket Club) at an "away" game 30 miles on from Boyup Brook, when we received the fire call over the Bush radio. The match was immediately abandoned and we all headed back for our farms as fast as we could. When we got past the Mayanup Hall on the gravel road we saw on the horizon to the right a broad front of flames advancing across the cleared and semi-cleared countryside. The bright red and orange flames seemed to fill the whole horizon in a wall of flame, and was rapidly approaching, seemingly devouring everything in its way. This was my first sight of a bushfire in Australia. The wall of flame was approaching rapidly and so Mark dropped off at the farm where he used to work to help the owner race around opening gates and cutting fences in the hopes that the sheep would head for the dams to escape. No time to drive them but just hope that they would find their way in front of the advancing flames. I continued driving home with the idea of getting Mark's sheepdog Floss, but it all happened so quickly, that the all-consuming flames had probably gone through the property before I even arrived back at Ardua. At home we set about moving our sheep into safer areas, with dams, for them to hopefully go to should the flames reach our property. What none of us newcomers realised at the time was the speed and ferocity of such a blaze on such a day and how total the devastation could be.

Fortunately for us, 19 miles away from the fire front, the wind changed. Western Australia has what they call the Fremantle Doctor, which is a breeze that generally comes in from the south-west mid-afternoon in the summer. This wind change took the advancing fire away from us.

One of the locals, an old farmer aged 80 odd, sat on his wooden veranda at the front of his basic wooden shack that he had built. He looked out over the long grass up to the veranda floorboards and the dry khaki paddocks beyond full of dead trees and said, "the wind will change!" And sure enough it did! The fire burned back on itself and the firefighters were able to contain it that evening, one mile down the road from him.

However there were several anxious days before it was totally under control. Apparently the fire had begun on a farm where a petrol engine was started up to pump some water. On that sort of day there would have been a total ban on small engines and on moving tractors or machinery in paddocks - for a very good reason. The whole of the Mayanup district was decimated with total sheep and cattle losses; burnt out fences; and complete feed destruction. It is not so much the sheep and cattle getting burnt to death - it is the swiftness of the fire through the grass and clover that burns their feet, and the bellies of the sheep. They are left there standing and suffering. The whole district spent days shooting the animals and digging big pits in which to bury them in. Some of this stock had taken years of breeding for specific micron of wool production, or carcass size and breeding qualities. This was a huge setback for the farmers' breeding programme.

The mateship of the Aussie is an awesome thing to see in action and the surrounding districts all buckled in to help (as they always did and are still doing). Teams of volunteers from all walks of life came down from Perth and all around the State, to help with the clearance and erection of new fences. Farmers in other districts provided fodder for the animals that had survived; agistment on their land until fences were erected or until the winter rains came and provided food and comfort to those so badly affected.

The whole affair was a shock and wake-up call to us newbies on how ready and prepared we had to be. Firefighting equipment and access to water, and fire control plans had to be a priority in case such an eventuality should occur again. This equipment nowadays on farms is much bigger and more efficient, with huge capacity water carrying tanks, and engines with bigger, faster pumping capability. In the days when we began farming, there used to be lookout towers at the top of big Karri and Jarrah trees in the forest that spotters radioed from if smoke was spotted. Nowadays there are aeroplanes aloft to undertake that warning lookout role. However, clearing and developing land is not so prevalent nowadays, but fire is still a huge factor in Australia. In the summers our drier climates and hotter temperatures are resulting in more combustion than ever before. Dad always used to say that the best form of attack on Australia would be to set the country alight! Nature seems to be doing that in this modern era!

Main Shearing

The shearing day is quite a regimented affair as the shearers work extremely hard in two hour stretches at a time for an eight-hour day, with two half-hour tea breaks and an hour for lunch. A typical shearing day starts at 7.30am - shearing until 9.30 - then a half hour break called "smokoe" for a mug of tea, sausage rolls, sandwiches and biscuits or slices. On the dot of 10am back to the shearing board for another two hours and then knock off for an hour for lunch which is a main meal and dessert. Back to the shearing board for another two-hour stint before the afternoon smokoe at 3pm., when again there is a mug of tea, more sandwiches and cakes. There is then a final two-hour stint before knocking off at 5.30pm.

As long as a sheep is caught in the holding pen and dragged onto the board before the second-hand ticks over to the final minute of the run a shearer can shear in it to push his tally figures up for that two- hour run. So, although the shearer knocks off on the dot, or soon after, the shed hand or "roustabout" as they are called, does not get his/her mug of tea and sandwiches until the fleece is thrown and skirted; the "board" swept clean, and the catching pens re-loaded with sheep to be shorn for the next run. Shearing time was a very pressured exercise with Mark doing the wool classing and skirting one side of the wool table with two shed hands (one being myself), to help on the table. Both shed hands pick up the shorn fleeces to be thrown on to the wool table and keep the shearing board swept. Keith and Dad were doing the wool pressing of the shorn fleeces and penning up the sheep to be shorn. Mum was the cook and bottle washer and kept extremely busy and on time supplying the food for us all.

We soon slotted into our various positions and although we were all frantically busy there were a lot of light-hearted moments involving the shearers and shed hands, to lighten the monotony of it all. I soon learnt that dropping the broom handle with a clatter meant a jug of beer! Then moving the belly wool out of the way quickly before the fleece wool started to be shorn made life a lot easier when the time came to pick up the fleece, all in one piece, and throw it onto the wool table. Sometimes a shearer would go to great lengths to hide the belly piece just for the hell of it! Occasionally, at the end of a run I would take the hand piece and finish off shearing the final leg of a sheep, under instructions, and it proved a useful skill to learn for later sheep husbandry at Ardua!

Shearing days started very early as we had to keep the sheep numbers up to the shearers. At the end of the day, we had to count the sheep out of each shearer's counting-out pen and return the shorn sheep to different paddocks. Then probably bring in another mob to be shorn which sometimes entailed drafting lambs from them and then shedding the sheep. We also confined other woolly sheep underneath the shed if the weather was at all unsettled, as fleeces must be dry when being shorn, for the handpiece combs and cutters to operate properly. There were usually quite a few wool bales to be topped up, pressed, stamped, and then stacked out of the way.

Although it was the culmination of one aspect of our year's endeavour and a major part of our annual income, we used to hate the regimentation of it all. It was very time-pressured constant work in the shed, on the farm and in the kitchen. However, we loved working with and handling the wool. The fibres in a moderately fine fleece have a lovely soft feel in the hands, and a beautiful brightness and clean, soft glow.

The actual shearing of a sheep is quite fascinating to watch as the shearer performs the smooth cutting action right on the sheep's skin and the whole fleece comes off virtually in one piece. The art of shearing is in having the sheep comfortably sitting up and leaning its back on the bent-over shearer. The right-handed shearer uses his left hand to sometimes immobilise muscles or pull the skin flat so that the hand piece glides over the contours of the body, maximizing the amount of wool that is evenly cut. As with all experts it is a pleasure to watch and is made to look so easy. The positioning of the sheep is almost constantly being altered so that the whole fleece comes off in virtually one piece. The rouseabout then learns to recognise the back legs, to pick one up in each hand and then throw the whole fleece onto the wool table in one quick action. This means it all holds together and looks like a sheep lying on its tummy. The shorter and dirty bits of wool are picked off around the edges and then the whole fleece is rolled up and put in a wool bale marked by stencil detailing the contents, destined for the auction floor or a contract with a private wool buyer. The price is determined by the weight and micron of the wool in the bale, and the determining factor of whether it is "fine" or "broad" in staple, or all points in between.

Fine merino wool makes up into such beautiful clothing that is both warm and cool, as it has a breathing quality that the synthetics do not possess, hence the expense. It also has durability and a quality appearance. Indeed "there is no substitute for wool" but perhaps we are slightly biased in saying that!

Most of the buyers nowadays are usually looking for a definite number of microns in Australian merino wool so that they can safely blend it with broader type wools to complete a specific order for a clothing manufacturer. The really broad types of wool (possessing low numbers on the micron scale) are usually from crossbred flocks of sheep and bought for making socks and carpets.

Rewards

There where rewards at the end of a hard day's work. Even the winters did not seem cold in those days. Sitting outside watching the shadows lengthen as the sun went down, with the sheep grazing the green pastures. Then the " Alpen Rosa" glow that briefly lit the whole scene in a rosy hue for ten minutes or so – making everything look picture perfect. We could not afford to drink beer, but used to buy flagons of medium dry sherry, and small glass of sherry at the end of the day, as a reward for all our hard work, made life seem pretty good and not to be swapped for the life we had left.

Sitting outside in the moonlight with the dark outlines of farm buildings and trees in the paddocks and with the full moon shining down out of the star-studded sky above with no haze of city lights to detract from the canopy of pure light and the endlessness of the firmaments above, somehow seemed to accentuate the pure size of the country in which we were now living.

The pure melodic sound of the magpies chorusing in the stillness and vastness of it all, with a metallic sound in the background now and again, as the frogs in the gully and dam below where we were sitting, echoed their tune in addition to the night noises around us. It was the vastness of it all that always struck me. A great amphitheatre of beauty that I had not experienced in England. Just as during the day, the vista over cleared paddocks with the sky above, perhaps with some clouds, or an unending blue canopy stretching to the horizon far in the distance, gave me the feeling of more spaciousness than I had ever experienced before. There seemed to be far more sky in Australia than in England, where the horizon was often covered by thick cloud that seemed to hang over you and minimise the horizon, whereas the spaciousness of the bush, land and sky was very striking because it seemed so much more distant and endless.

In the spring the leaves in the tops of the trees seemed to shimmer in the sunshine, as the gum in the leaves reflected the light in a magic way. The peace and quietness of it all, if there was no wind, echoed to the twittering chirps of little bird life around and the melodic chortling sounds of black and white magpies in the daytime. The iconic kookaburra seemed to start its maniacal laughter at any time of the day but at night-time it echoed through the darkness and seemed uncannier and more foreign to the peaceful surroundings, but the melodic crescendo of song from the magpies in the moonlight restored beauty and pure harmony to your senses.

Veggie Garden

Mum planted a veggie garden, and she certainly brought her green fingers from the many gardens she had started in the UK and also in France. She always did say that WA had the most difficult climate to adjust to for growing veggies that she ever had known. It was so hot and dry in the summer, necessitating a good watering system. In the winter we did have the occasional frost at Boyup and could sometimes cop one or two in the Spring to catch us unawares. There also seemed to be all sorts of bugs that could attack the plants, so local knowledge became a necessity and took quite a while to acquire.

Notwithstanding this, Mum grew lovely fresh green vegetables and potatoes. After a year or two we put in a beautiful big asparagus bed, starting with many barrow loads of sheep droppings buried deep below the ground, and then a lot of soil, with more sheep manure just under the topsoil. As the years passed sheep manure was never in short supply! Loganberry bushes were planted and trained onto the fence that was put up around the garden. We had beautiful cream we milked from our Jersey cow to go with all the delicious fruits as Mum also planted some fruit trees - peach, pear, nectarine, quince, mulberry, lemons, oranges and grapefruit - and then one English oak for posterity! We also had two Feijoa trees, and walnut trees. The previous owner had put in a passionfruit vine and two apricot trees, that as the years passed grew to be enormous trees with the most beautiful deep yellowy orange apricots that we enjoyed and look back on with nostalgia. So as can be imagined Mum and I were flat out bottling, jam making and preserving all these fruits in the summer.

We ensured a plentiful water supply from a dam that was put in on a hill in the paddock opposite, beyond the garden. An iconic windmill pumped the water from the dam into a concrete tank at ground level above the dam. That water flowed down by gravity to a tank up on a metal stand by the veggie garden, which then flowed down to various watering points. This tank also supplied water to a few troughs in nearby paddocks for the stock.

We had to share the fruit to a certain extent with the local birdlife, silver eyes and green parrots - who hung around to sample the ripening fruit. The parrots were very annoying as they nipped off the hard, unripe and soft fruit from the trees and then only sampled one or two bites from the fruit on the ground leaving the rest to rot. I am afraid we resorted to some lead with a .22 rifle to share crop with them!

Quite a few olive trees were also planted, both a pickling variety and one for oil. Alas pickling olives became too labour-intensive. It entailed soaking the olives in a brine that had to be drained off and renewed every day for quite a length of time before packing them in jars in the final brine. They tasted delicious but proved too much like the tedious labour and routine of the daily soaking of nappies and then washing them!

Mum even made her own soap for the washing machine with fat from the sheep, clarified, caustic soda, borax and some resin. This mixture was then cut into bars and could be used after a month, in the twin-tub washing machine we had invested in!

She proved so adaptable and very thrifty over the years, but of course she came from Scottish descent!

So, what with the home-killed mutton; home-grown veggies; our own milk and butter, our own orchard and preserved fruits, we lived very cheaply and very well, and our monetary needs were very basic and limited, which was just as well as the clearing costs proved very high. We were desperate to develop the land to carry sheep and sow income generating crops – but still the bank overdraft was mounting up and interest rates were rising.

Sheep Husbandry

Sheep husbandry took up a large proportion of our time. Wool and meat were two of our major sources of income, but also provided a fair proportion of our annual expenses and hours of work at certain times of the year. Aside from the expertise of shearing which we contracted out basically once a year, we ourselves did the crutching. This entailed taking some wool off the rear end of a sheep with a shearing hand piece to keep it clean, around six months before shearing. We also did some dagging, if a sheep had urine and excreta staining just before shearing, but this was not always necessary. This operation was purely to ensure that there was the minimum of stained wool and lumps of "dags" (faeces) coming off with the fleece wool.

There was also the dipping of the sheep after shearing, running them through a sheep shower to provide reasonable long-term protection against blowflies. Over the years this dipping action was replaced and the shower dispensed with. Protection was achieved by just applying a backliner on the backs of the sheep in a race, which was quicker to do, with less hardship on the sheep and the operator!

We very often had to draft sheep into various mobs, depending on their age; or whether they were going to be moved to a different plane of feed because they were in lamb. Others were going to be served by Merino rams for wool production or Border Leicester rams to produce fat lambs for the meat market. We also had to sometimes drench the sheep to protect them against intestinal worms.

We usually had our main lamb drop in the winter in the months of June/July when there was hopefully some good green clover and grass in the paddocks, and this then produced the additional stock work of marking and tailing the progeny. We had a lamb marking cradle which rotated on a spindle in the centre. Five of us would then position ourselves around the cradle with different jobs to perform. The first person would catch out of a small pen, lift the lamb, and lie it on its back with the hind legs stretched out and clipped in position. Then the cradle was rotated one position to the second operator who would operate a syringe needle containing protection against pulpy kidney disease. The next rotation was for the third person in position to apply a rubber ring to the purse (if a male sheep – to neuter it), and finally use an instrument to clip an ear mark and coloured tag into one of the animal's ears, to denote which gender the lamb was. The cradle was then spun on its final rotation for a ring on the tail, or the use of a "hot knife" to cut the tail off and let the lamb out. It was a very synchronized operation overall, and we used to get through over 500 lambs in the day, according to the number of ewes in the mob. So, as you can imagine, our dogs had quite a work-out too.

About a month later we would bring the ewes and lambs in again; draft the lambs off and drench all the lambs with slow-release pellets of selenium to aid their future growth. The late lambs in the mob were dealt with as before.

We often had to feed out oats and perhaps lupins to the sheep at the break of season to supplement the green feed which was struggling to emerge after sparse rainfall. In later years we often had to start feeding the ewes before we had had any rain, as the weather pattern has changed.

I or one of the kids would drive the ute with Mark perched on the back with the bags of feed and lay a trail of oats or lupins on the ground in the paddock for the sheep to eat. He always used to joke to our visitors that it was very biblical "I know my sheep and my sheep know me!" as he called them up in the paddock and they came running! Little did the visitors know that at the sound of the ute they would all come running as they were ever-hopeful of food! He used to wonder why it didn't work with me!

We bought a feeder bin later, which we towed with the ute and this was much quicker and a one-person job - and the sheep still all came running!

GWEN and KIWI

Gwen and Kiwi, great friends of Mark's parents, had retired from the Air Force to live in Perth WA. They had all first met when in India before World War II, where Dad was flying on the Northwest frontier and Kiwi was the young local doctor on the same station. As often happened in the Royal Air Force they had renewed their friendship in various postings over the years. They were also great friends of my parents and Kiwi was my father's boss as the principal medical officer (PMO) at Fighter Command, (where Mark's Dad was the Commander-in-chief as it happened!), and later again at Second TAF in Germany.

When Mark's parents were in India Kiwi recommended to Mum that she take their eldest son Keith to Sydney Australia to live with her sister and husband for a couple of years as the Indian climate did not suit him. Mark's birth was imminent and so he was born whilst she was in Australia. Mark says he only stayed three weeks as he didn't like the place! But it always provided the answer when he was accused of being a Pom because of his English accent. He would say in a lofty voice "Well actually I was born in Sydney, Australia, as was my mother and so I am actually a second-generation Aussie, what are you?!"

At the end of his career Kiwi had returned to WA to take up medicine again in Perth and so the friendships were renewed, and we saw a lot of them before we got married. They very kindly stood in for my parents who were unable to come out for our wedding. They had sadly lost a daughter at birth in India, around the time that Mark was born, and so it was even more special and meaningful for Kiwi to accompany me up the long aisle at St Mary's Cathedral in Perth to give me away. They even lent their house for our small wedding reception and of course continued the friendship with us all over the years.

We often stayed with them on trips to Perth even after some of our kids had come along and my parents enjoyed the renewal of their friendship and hospitality as they flew in and out on their many trips to WA to see us all.

Job & Marriage

I rented a very basic bedroom, with access to a shared bathroom and kitchen, in a rather insalubrious part of Perth, over the railway from the city centre. The rental suited me as I could walk to my secretarial job for the four months before we got married, and my salary added to our meagre savings before the wedding. I worked for a lawyer in St George's Terrace in the tallest building in the city at that time, which was probably eight storeys in height! Slightly different to the skyscrapers that adorn the city skyline nowadays!

I hated being away from the farm and found the job extremely boring. However, as a means to an end I stuck it out, not seeing Mark very often and only knowing a couple of people then in Perth to start with. However, I joined a ladies' cricket team, although I can't even remember the name of the Club now!
I was heartily glad when I could return to the farm for the few weeks before our wedding and help Mark finish off getting our caravan habitable.

We had a very small wedding, which meant a very long walk with Kiwi Corbet down the lengthy aisle of St Mary's Catholic Cathedral to the small congregation of family and friends at the front altar, but it was very special of course!

We borrowed Dad's A70 shooting brake for the honeymoon, whilst they had a cramped journey back to the farm in Keith's little A40 Ute. But when we came to leave the hotel the following morning, we could only go in reverse! So, we had to beg a bed from our very good spinster friend Dilly for two nights, before we could head South in the repaired vehicle! We had two weeks touring a bit of the Southwest of the State sticking to the coast-line as much as possible and camping in a tent which blew down on us at times, and eventually returned to take up married bliss in our "new to us" little abode – the caravan! And back to work!

Black Cattle

The decision had been made to buy in some black Angus cattle from a local farmer about a year after taking over the farm. They were acknowledged as a breed that were "good doers" in the South-west of Western Australia. In retrospect we surmised that these particular ones were being culled from his property as they were flighty and in danger of leading the rest of his herd astray. Wooden cattle yards were built with the aid of the working gang, by felling trees and digging holes with the posthole digger on the tractor for the solid wooden uprights for the yards and wooden railings that were bought from one of the nearby sawmills. We had erected a very good boundary fence around the property, but our internal fencing was really only suitable for sheep at best and merino sheep at that. Merinos tended to run as a mob and normally were not really adventurous! But our crossbred sheep, bred from merino ewes crossed with a Border Leicester ram to develop a fat lamb flock, tended to test their boundaries especially if there was better feed over the fence! And of course the cattle did this even more so!

We had spent a fair bit of time trying to control these cattle. In the end we tired of trying to chase them through the uncleared blocks on the farm, back to where they should be. This finally sealed their fate and after a couple of years or so they eventually left the farm on a truck. There was one steer that proved really elusive to catch. So, we enlisted the help of one of our neighbouring farmers with his rifle and eventually cornered the steer and shot him. We hung the carcass up on the front blade of the tractor and butchered up the carcass the next day, packing the meat in the freezers of our refrigerators. I missed out on the butchering episode as I was nine months pregnant with our first baby. A day of walking and running throughout the day through the bush, trying to corner the runaway, hastened the arrival of our first son, after our 30-mile drive into the hospital into town that evening!

The steer meant that we had to eat solid beef for the next few months, as we had no room to store a sheep carcass as well in the freezers, but it was a refreshing change to our mutton diet! However, we did conclude that there are many more ways of cooking a sheep, rather than an unadulterated diet of beef!

Early Days of Marriage

When we got married, we had bought this second-hand old 14-foot caravan to be our abode and stripped it down inside. We bought a kitchen set-up (cupboards, bench tops and sink) from a caravan maker in Perth, and Mark's parents gave us a full size four burner gas stove with oven for a wedding present) which ran on bottled gas, (equivalent to calor gas in the UK). We then had a couple of small wardrobe cupboards plus a dining area at the other end of the van, with bench cushions each side of a table that folded down at night. The cushions, on top of the folded down table, formed our double bed at night with lockers under the cushions for the bedding. This meant of course that we had to make up the bed every night! We built a cover over the van with four bush poles and a tin roof to shield the van from the worst of the sun in the summer and winter rains. We also had a small, corrugated iron shed next to the caravan which housed the fridge run on kerosene (paraffin in the UK).

This abode was pulled up outside the shack (Buckingham Palace) which was a spare room until the kids came along. They shared this room until number four arrived, so it was basic living for eight years! We planted a small lawn outside the van and the shack, so it was really quite civilised, but very outdoor living for all of us.

The kids came in for meals but were then encouraged to head outside to play. If the weather was inclement once they were old enough they would go over to the wool shed to amuse themselves. There they had plenty of room to run around and play tag or jump around the wool bales dodging a thrown tennis ball, plus other games they devised. The bookworm of the family could be found comfortably lying on some fleeces of wool reading a book whilst bedlam was going on around her! Otherwise, it was into their bedroom in the shack. This outdoor living was very possible because of the climate we have in WA. They could just put on an extra jumper or jacket if it was cold. The children were often out in the paddock with us during the day, as the work programme continued, so their play area there was a really big one!

The current baby would be outside too! We had a strong cane pram with a big hood, and the babies loved being under the trees in the little orchard alongside the shack, watching the branches and leaves dancing in the breeze, but being snuggly sheltered and warm or cool depending on the season, with a net over the pram to keep the flies away. Watching the chooks (hens) was also a fascinating occupation for the current baby, so not much wonder they all had lovely complexions! Of course, the grandchildren often spent time with Mark's mother, helping her to make rock buns and cook cakes, as she was very generous with her time and home space.

My Dad had taken study leave from the RAF to undertake a tropical medicine course at Edinburgh university. He then had the good fortune of being posted to Singapore twice over a few years.

I flew over there for a holiday with our first-born son Paul, when he was a year old, and they then flew over to WA to see exactly what Australia looked like, and what we were up to there. Although they had had copious letters describing the scene and our way of life, I think they were still surprised and fairly shocked at our primitive life and the conditions! They had to share our son's bedroom in Buckingham Palace. Fortunately he was a very good sleeper, whilst the current baby (our eldest daughter) was in her bassinet in the caravan. Of course, the cushions of our bed were the seats at the table during the day, so while we had dinner in the evening, she was relegated to the big cane pram in the nearby shed. My mother said, "the rats will eat that baby!" But we assured her that wouldn't happen as that is why we kept cats!

A few years later they were again in Singapore, and they managed to hitch a ride on an RAF Hercules aircraft, flying from RAF Changi to Perth WA. Imagine the faces of our five children when they lobbed into WA with four bikes and a trike in the hold of the huge aeroplane!

How to Get on Well
with Your In-Laws

Living in the caravan did not afford the luxury of something so simple as drying and airing nappies after our first born arrived. So Mark's parents were very good and allowed me to air the nappies by the '" Wonder-heat "fire in their kitchen of the cottage when they were not around. They had gone to Perth, and Keith had come down to the caravan for a meal with us. I had inadvertently put the clothes horse too close to the fire. When Keith returned after the meal and opened the door of the kitchen he was greeted with black smoke and just about passed out from the fumes.

The smouldering nappies had been suffocated by the fumes of the foam rubber seating on the kitchen chairs, as had the skirting board around the kitchen - so mercifully the fire had gone out! Alas, the burnt melted black rubber from the chairs was stuck to all the furniture and walls and worse still to the original oil painting that hung over the heater. The painting had to go to the West Australian Art Gallery to be restored and given a new frame.

Mark's parents were so understanding and forgiving of the whole episode - even to the extent of giving us some of the insurance money to buy new nappies! Of course this meant more privations and hardship for them, as they had to vacate their kitchen and again use the Tilley lamps and camp stove on the verandah as the kitchen got refurbished. But they did get painters and plasterers in on the insurance payout to do the work, so it was not too lengthy a process. Dad very typically and generously said they were intending to do a re-painting job of the kitchen sometime anyway!

Basically, Dad was quite happy working physically most of the time, but he also seemed to have a mountain of correspondence to deal with every mail day, which was three times a week. He did enjoy watching Mark at Boyup Brook and in later years his youngest son Paddy at Cape Riche playing cricket sometimes. Mum got involved with the local girl guide community at one stage and ended up as the District Commissioner for a year or two, so she got involved with the locals to a certain degree. Not that she was being standoffish - she just concentrated more on working on the farm and in the garden and being there with Dad. I suppose she had never had a driving licence and so it was difficult for her to be independently involved off the farm.

But of course they were invited to various official functions up in Perth at Government House over the years. The annual Battle of Britain function and Remembrance Day; the visit of the Queen and the Duke of Edinburgh, and other official functions and visits by people Dad had worked with or entertained whilst in the Air Force. They also flew over to RAAF Tengah in Malaysia for a week to attend the final closing down of one of the RAF squadrons that Dad had commanded during the war, and that gave them a very welcome break and a real holiday.

A couple of the State Governors were in the RAF and like Dad had flown regularly on missions against the enemy, so Mum and Dad greatly enjoyed catching up with them on a fairly regular basis and doubtless a few tales would have been swapped over the after-dinner brandies! The WA Governor in

Dad's latter years was West Australian born Digger Kyle and indeed his nephew farmed in WA, not far from the family at the second farm at Cape Riche.

This Governor had flown throughout the war and knew Mum and Dad extremely well. He asked if he and his wife could be of any help to Dad who then asked them if we could park our cars in the grounds of Government House when in Perth as we had trouble finding parking sites within the centre of the city and they were very expensive. He very generously offered parking facilities in the grounds at the back of Government House.

We hoped he was not too embarrassed when Dad once rolled up with two ceramic pedestals and toilet bowls highly embarrassingly obvious in the back of his ute!

Visitors

Over the years we had various visitors to the farm at Boyup Brook.One of Dad's greatest friends in the RAF was an Australian who decided to jump on a ship and head over to Britain to join the RAF as a pilot early in the war. He used to stay with Mum and Dad on the odd occasion of a day off flying operations and indeed they hosted the wedding of Mac and his English wife when they got married. He was always very popular with Mark who knew him to be what he imagined a "dinkum Aussie" looked like, tall and sunburnt, with a laconic manner and an Australian drawl. When Mark asked him "did he have a boomerang?" Mac replied "no, but he would bring one the next time he visited" and true to his word he made a boomerang and presented it to this little seven-year-old boy on his next visit. It flew, and it came back to the thrower!

Mac flew operationally with Dad during the war in the Mosquito squadron that Dad commanded. On Operation Jericho, just before the Allied landing in Normandy, Mac was shot down and spent the rest of the war in a German prison camp. Whilst there his engineering skills were put to good use making wire cutters out of ice skates and other tools to help escaping prisoners. As you can imagine they had many yarns to swap when they met up again in Boyup Brook on the farm.

Mac ran a very successful engineering company in Melbourne and had retained his pilot's licence through the years and regularly flew his two aeroplanes - a four-seater Beechcraft and a 10-seater Queen Air. He hired these planes out frequently. He had also invested in quality cars, owning two Rolls Royces and an Aston Martin. He reckoned that the cars held their value and were a better investment than having money in the Bank! He drove his powder blue Rolls-Royce right across the Nullarbor to visit his close friends, Hope and Basil Embry, to see what they were up to on the other side of the continent. He greatly enjoyed his visit, as did we all, and it very much tickled our fancy to go to the local drive-in cinema thirty miles away one evening in the Rolls. That must have been the first and last time in the whole of WA - or indeed Australia- that a Rolls Royce was seen at a drive-in!!!

Whilst he was over in the West he sussed out a possible landing strip on our farm for his smaller aeroplane, which entailed opening a fence for the plane to land in one paddock and run through the gap into the next one. It proved plenty long enough for the landing, but his wife mildly had kittens as all she could see from where she was sitting, behind the pilot, was the landing aircraft taxiing into a fence on either side of the aeroplane the first time they used the strip! Mum and Dad had quite a few flights whilst Mac was with them, and they would both have enjoyed being airborne again and especially Dad with the chance to keep his hand in at the controls. Mac also came over with a plane full of passengers to see the new acquisition of the farm at Cape Riche in later years, but he had to use the local airstrip in Boyup for the bigger aircraft when they all came to see us. He had no trouble when Dad moved down South as the paddocks were bigger and a local farmer had put in an airstrip for himself that Mac was able to use.

Another couple of visitors were from the UK. Dad went to Bromsgrove School in Worcestershire and had kept in touch with the old school matron. She had obviously followed Dad's Air Force career and knew what he was doing, and she came out to see just what he was up to in his retirement. The matron was well in her eighties, and her younger sister an octogenarian also. Dad drove them down from Perth in Keith's little A40 Ute as his A 70 shooting brake was out of action at the time. He put a camping armchair in the back of the ute for the younger sister and the matron sat in the front and she was so little that we could barely see her head over the dashboard as they drove into the farm! But they were both in raptures about the drive, the scenery, and the adventure of it all!

Feeding Lambs

We milked a cow or sometimes bought in powdered milk to feed the orphan lambs with a bottle in the early days. We would wrap the lambs in old woollens and keep them in a cardboard box by the wood stove in Buckingham Palace. Later they were kept in the kitchen of the cottage where the "Wonderheat" wood-burning heater provided the warmth. It also had a flat top where there would always be a big kettle heating water, and often a big pot of soup slowly cooking away.

We even had a pet kangaroo once, hanging beside the stove in a hessian bag which was stuffed with old woollens to keep it warm. Its mother had been tragically shot and so it was brought out of the pouch to be hopefully reared. It had to be fed with a very special formula, via a very small tube in a bottle and was quite difficult to rear and we had no success with quite a few of them. However, we did rear one, years later, when we were living in our house, after we had our family. It was a great pet and used to hop inside and stand beside the cupboard where the peanuts were kept! In the hopes because she really liked them!

Quite often Mum would be wearing her pearl earrings when feeding the lambs, which we always remarked upon as looking pretty classy!

We went round the lambing paddocks during the flush couple of months of lambing; sometimes to help lamb-down ewes having difficulties, but we tried to assist in any birth very quickly and then vamoose the scene as fast as possible leaving the ewe to mother up with the lamb. We discovered Merino ewes are very flighty creatures and notorious for heading off from the scene and leaving their newborn as though they had never had it. Consequently, we then preferred to watch the process through binoculars and not interfere unless we had to, after considering whether other ewes were nearby who might miss-mother if we came too close to them.

Feeding orphan lambs could be quite expensive if we were not milking a cow. It could also be quite time-consuming; losses could be quite high and it was hard to justify the time taken during the clearing programme days - so we gave it away in the end.

We did however have quite a bit of success "mothering-on" an orphan lamb if a ewe had lost her lamb at birth. We would bring the ewe in and shut her in a small pen with an orphan lamb on which we had draped the skin off her dead lamb. The smell of the skin often fooled the ewe into accepting the substitution.

Naturally our small children loved the pet lambs and being involved with them! Indeed, one of our young daughters had to be banned from the lambing paddocks! She would spot a young lamb lying in the sun in the winter, with no mother visible nearby as the ewe was away in the paddock having a good feed (and enjoying a bit of peace and quiet no doubt!) Our daughter would proudly come home with the "abandoned" lamb to mother and keep as a pet lamb! She was then sent back post haste to drop the lamb where she had found it in the hopes that the ewe had not returned meanwhile. In the end we had to issue instructions that she was not to venture near the lambing paddocks unless she was with an adult!

Cash Crops

Gradually the clover areas had sheep grazing on them and so they were no longer pure enough for our clover sales. So we were then on the lookout for other money-making to pay the costs for our continued clearing programme. The lupin seed market was a lucrative one and as has been said also supplemented the ongoing fertility of our soils. The bitter blue lupins that we used to grow in the very early years of our development had been superseded by the new varieties of yellow and white flowering lupins and these were suitable for human consumption. They were also a very good high protein stockfeed when harvested and when the stubble was grazed afterwards. The University of WA carried out experimental seedings on Ardua and so we were in on the growing and sale of these new varieties very early on in their development.

We also sowed vetch seed to be harvested and sold as a seed crop. This provided excellent grazing protein, especially for young sheep, as did the stubble when the vetch crop was taken off.

We did however have a challenge growing the purple vetches one year. We always had to spray the vetch crop against cut worm infestations before harvest and we noticed our magnificent vetch plants were suddenly curling up their toes and dying. The manager of the company that sold the spray came down to the farm and struck up quite a friendship with Dad. It was discovered that the spray used from the drums had been affected by some contaminated mixture in them and that had caused the devastation. The company compensated us for the loss of the crop, but of course we missed out on the bonus additional advantage we usually had of grazing our weaned lambs on the stubble. All numbered batches of that chemical that had been distributed around the State were re-called.

Imagine our horror and that of the chemical company when it happened again the following year! The company manager could not believe it and it nearly ended a beautiful friendship! However, they concluded that the culprit drums must have been at the back of some agricultural shed and missed out on the recall, so they again compensated us. Dad did think about ringing the company manager the following year! - but thought perhaps not as it might have given him a heart attack!

Kangaroos

Kangaroos could be a real menace on our farm, surrounded by bush as most of it was. They came in from the forest (bush) to eat our sheep feed and crops. They were dynamite on our fences, pushing under the netting or jumping into and over the top. As we were virtually surrounded by bush, it meant that roos could come in in quite big numbers at night-time.

Driving on roads through the bush especially at dusk or night could be quite hazardous. We had to keep a very sharp eye on movements just off the sides of the road or in the bush as the headlights seemed to attract the kangaroos and they tended to jump out across the road. And if you saw one – there were probably two or three close on its heels.

Most vehicles had an iron roo bar to protect the radiator and front of the vehicle, but it was inevitable to have some roo damage over the years. We learnt where the worst spots were on the road to and from town and that we also had to go really slowly once we entered our property over the cattle grid, especially looking from left to right, where the roos could launch themselves off a bank running alongside the road for a mile or so! We also had some trouble in the paddocks with emus. They proved murderous on the fences – just attacking them and trampling the netting and wires down. Fortunately, there were less of them, and they generally moved on when chased and harassed by our sheepdogs.

We used to spotlight and shoot kangaroos for dog tucker, going out at night in the ute, with two people standing in the back. One person held the spotlight and directed it around to illuminate the kangaroos in the paddock and the second person used the .22 rifle or a shot gun. It sounds cruel but there were so many of them damaging fences, trampling them down and eating our crops and it was a fact of life that our two or three sheepdogs needed feeding. (But it did seem rather incongruous to be shooting the national emblem of Australia!) Actually, the haunches of a young kangaroo proved very tender when roasted, and the tail proved very edible, similar to an oxtail in soups or casserolesoles.

For a year or two after taking over the farm we had a spate of roo shooters in their utes with spotlights searching for roos as they drove on the road through our property and round the fire breaks outside our fences. Of course, this was dangerous to our sheep in the paddocks alongside the road, not ideal for lambing ewes especially as the noise of the gunshots scattered them in the paddock and could have caused serious miss-mothering or frightened them through fences.

This lawlessness was anathema to Dad who would hear the shots and immediately leap out of bed into action, summoning Keith who lived with them. As they ran down to the shed past the caravan, they called to Mark to join them in the car. Then off they would set at a rate of knots, with no lights showing, as they wanted to surprise the roo shooters in the act! They never caught them though as the roo shooters probably deviated off at one of the many forestry tracks through the bush, and after a while they did not bother us anymore.

But I think Dad quite enjoyed "the chase!" However, the boys weren't quite so sure - as speeding down a dirt road with no lights on was slightly hairy to say the least!

Years later when the new road was being pushed through the bush on one end of our farm there were a lot of bulldozers and earth moving equipment on our far boundary as they knocked the timber over to push through the new road, and the workers camped out on the job. We knew the workers shot kangaroos in the bush outside the farm but usually on dusk or at night under spotlights. One morning I was walking up to the cottage and I suddenly felt a rush of wind past my right ear. Dad was some distance away, but he instantly recognised the crack noise from a .303 rifle and twigged very quickly what was happening. He straight away ran for the car and drove off at a rate of knots to confront them. They probably wondered what had hit them when he caught up with them!

I hadn't really realised quite what had happened and that the sudden rush of wind was of a bullet flying past my ear. I was just so thankful that our current little two-year-old on my left hip had not been on the right one, as she would have collected that bullet without a doubt! And also, how lucky had I been!

Change of Land Boundaries

Dad used his diplomatic skills and personality to make deals with the WA Lands Department to straighten up some of our farm boundaries to make the fencing more cost-effective and for easier running of our stock. We relinquished some isolated blocks to the Forestry Department to straighten up some of our fence lines and suggested that some of our cleared acreage alongside Forestry bush where the State was pushing the new road through, be exchanged for the roadway that ran through the middle of our property. Ownership of the road through the farm meant we had a private raceway right through a lot of the farm and did not have strangers and roo shooters invading our space anymore. We also put in various cattle grids which cut down on our fencing costs and made life easier.

Building Our House

Our family was burgeoning and so Dad then decided it was time to give us a bit more space and freedom of movement and build his second house!

He ordered grey cement blocks this time, which were twice the size of small bricks which did prove quicker to put up than the red bricks he had used for the cottage, and of course he was more experienced this time.

We would generally do a concrete mix early in the morning before we went out to the paddocks, and this would set Dad up to get right into it with the building trowel! Mind you on one or two occasions we did find the wall he was working on had decreased in height by the end of that day which was a bit disheartening to me!

The plan was to build a three-bedroom house with an entry hall that we could use as a lounge to start with, and a bathroom with toilet, bath and shower leading off this lounge. When this was finished, we towed the caravan up and parked it parallel to the hall/lounge entrance. We still continued to use the kitchen and dining area to cook and eat in, in the caravan.

A small room leading from the outside through a door on this same wall housed a wood bath heater, two wash troughs and joy of joy a bigger washing machine for use by the two households, plus our electric fridge/ freezer. There was also shelving for stores and the copious jars of preserved fruit and jams that Mum and I bottled every summer.

We then actually owned a second-hand lounge suite and joy of joys the luxury of sleeping in a proper bed which we didn't have to make up every night! Plus, a bathroom with all mod cons with even a bath as well as the shower. We moved just before our fourth child was born, so now our three girls shared the bedroom. When our second boy arrived later, the two boys shared the second bedroom, and we occupied the smallest one.

The block of land on which the house was built sloped down slightly towards the shearing shed. The height of the house was quite considerable at one end and the corresponding height of the roof line necessitated some serious scaffolding poles; long straight Jarrah ones set well into the ground which came from trees felled on the property. Luckily Dad always seemed to have a good head for heights, but it meant some serious heavy lifting of the blocks and mortar to complete the job. A fairly steep pitched roof was designed, and Mark welded up the metal for the roof trusses holding the solid wooden bearers for the concrete tiles that roofing specialists completed.

Our local doctor who helped to bring four of our five children into the world was one of the Rats of Tobruk. He and Dad used to enjoy sharing time and stories together. The doctor and his wife came out to the farm one evening to see the progress on the building of our house, and they all enjoyed a meal together, and he and Dad enjoyed a very special bottle of whisky that Dad had been given which was very pure and high proof. So they were fairly merry by the end of the evening!

When the time came for them to depart Ted said, "Now what about this house you are building Basil – show me what you have done." Walking over to the half-built structure in the moonlight Ted handled a stack of masonry blocks waiting to be used in the construction and said: "Oh this is not too steady Basil – you'll have to do better than this!"

It was a great day when we towed the caravan up beside the house and moved in and it seemed such a palatial dwelling after what we had been used to over the years!

This abode served us well for a few years. Then of course priorities changed at Boyup Brook as we started to be involved further Southeast in the State with our share cropping ventures. We then got involved with our development of the Cape Riche end of Ardua in a separate farming venture, so all money and labour efforts were concentrated on these necessary new adventures!

Adding Onto Our House

After we had been occupying the house for two years or so, we decided we could add on a temporary kitchen/dining area, built as a lean-to on the entire end of the existing house to again cope with the increasing sizes of our five children! We employed a local builder to complete this addition as Dad was down South at Cape Riche building his third house down there!

This then meant that the two doors leading into the existing lounge and laundry became internal doors. We already had the two side walls built with the masonry blocks for the eventual finishing off from the kitchen/dining area. We used corrugated iron sloping down from the existing blocked-off tiled roof to a newly erected temporary "Hardie-plank wall". This "wall" was using the successor material to asbestos in Australia and extended the total width of the house. Then tongued and grooved timber floor finished off the room.

Our caravan, which had served us so well for seven years, was sadly but thankfully dispensed with! But nothing ever got wasted at Ardua, and the kids reduced it to just the chassis with sledgehammers and great gusto. It was then transformed into a trailer for a fire-fighting tank, equipped with a small engine.

The full-size bottled gas stove came out of the caravan, as did the kitchen cupboards which were a bit narrow and small, but very serviceable still, and with a new coat of paint looked almost new again! A new, full-sized kitchen sink with a big cupboard underneath was installed, and a decent -sized dining table and chairs at the other end of the long room made life easier for our growing children!

The crowning glory was a dishwasher on wheels that my mother-in-law gave me as a birthday present – because she said I needed one for our big family! So typical of her thoughtfulness and giving nature when she had gone without for so long.

Wool Stockpile

ustralia had had the enviable reputation of riding on the sheep's backs over the years. This country produced and supplied more than 80% of the world's apparel wool with farmers enjoying a return of 1 pound sterling per 1 pound of wool during the years of the Korean War. In fact people were ripping open their mattresses to sell the wool in them! But those false prices could not last once peacetime came about. When we started stocking the farm with sheep and selling wool the Chinese were the major buyers of the Australian clip. They purchased a small amount of "fine micron" softer type of wool for the Australian fashion industry. They also bought bigger quantities of the "broader micron" type of wool, which had a coarser feel to it, used in the making of cheaper clothing, such as working jumpers and carpets. We all used to joke that if every Chinaman bought one pair of socks, we the sheep farmers would be very happy and well off!

Bales of wool were either sold on farm or transported to the auction floor and bid on by different buyers, either local or from other countries. The different styles of wool always fluctuated in price according to the market demand. When we were developing the farm and always had big clearing costs, we usually had to accept the going price for the sale of our wool on the auction floor. By the time shearing came around we needed the money to pay our bills, as very often we were maxed up to the hilt on our overdraft with the bank. This meant we could not pay all our bills until the proceeds of the wool clip had come in!

The auction price of wool was then good, but when the market fell, instead of accepting the market price some businessmen bonded together to create the Wool Corporation to prop up an artificial floor price. This meant the sale of wool was no longer under the free auction system and the principal of free enterprise. There was then a tremendous loss of buyer confidence worldwide.

We woolgrowers questioned this interventionist system under the Wool Corporation, thus, manipulating a false floor price, resulting in buyer resistance. Huge stockpiles of unsold wool gradually built up around the country and we, the woolgrowers, were paying the price of rising costs and inability to store or get rid of our product. The Wool Corporation then created a wool levy on us all, to the tune of 25% on each growers' clip, to cover their costs. So not only could we not sell our wool, and had to store it, we had to pay this tax!

Their next brainwave was that we had to reduce the total amount of wool being produced in the country to 350 billion kilos. So, woolgrowers were then paid to reduce our flock numbers by shooting surplus sheep – with the taxpayer footing our meagre compensation bill! (Bearing in mind that the meat marketing system had also collapsed – so sending surplus sheep to the market resulted in a bill for cartage and auction costs but no dollars in our pockets!) You can imagine how terrible and heart rending this decision was to most farmers who like us were nurturing and improving their breeding program over the years, and who genuinely cared for the animals they ran on their land. We had to dig big pits and bury the carcasses.

This callous decision lay at the door of the Wool Corporation not the government.

The Federal Government then stopped guaranteeing the financial borrowings of the Wool Corporation and there was one of the worst business collapses ever to happen in Australia, resulting in a $12 billion loss to what had been the flagship industry for years! The whole sorry business ended up with banks foreclosing on farmers' borrowings and mortgage sales were abundant. Of course, the whole sheep industry suffered, as there was then a glut of sheep up for sale in the stockyards, their worth was minimal and there were no buyers around. The wool trade and the meat trade were in the doldrums for many years, and it took us on Ardua quite a few years to recover our liquidity and pay off the bank debt.

Share Cropping

Once most of Boyup Brook was cleared and productive, the challenge was to continue to gain extra income as the farm could not really support four families. We desperately needed to expand our ability to make more money, and of course the cost of clearing Ardua Boyup Brook had been more than we had bargained for. Ideally of course we would have liked to increase our acreage there but recognised that we needed to find a cheaper- to-develop area to buy into. To reconnoitre availability and suitability of more acreage we decided to do some share cropping down in the South of WA, East of Albany. This entailed the farmer owning all the land, providing the cost of the seed and superphosphate fertiliser, with us providing all machinery, fuel and labour and then splitting the profits fifty-fifty.

We chose one wheat growing area in an older, more settled area of the State with chocolate brown heavier country with more proven crop yields and a more reliable early break to the season. The second area we chose was in newer-established, lighter land that had some sandy soil, but more recently cleared in what was known as a" soldier settlement" area. These were acreages, with a basic house, that the government had made available to" returned servicemen" after the war, on generous terms and paid for over a period of years. Our plan was to work up and sow the heavier land before too much rain; followed by the lighter land which we hoped would not bog out too soon as the annual rainfall there was a lot less.

This meant taking a lot of our equipment down. Our second - hand Austin truck was put to good use taking most of the gear down in several trips - tractors, plough, combine seeder etc. The David Brown tractor towed the Claas header down at a speed of 8 kilometres per hour which meant Mark, who had drawn the short straw for the job from his brothers, left the Boyup farm at daylight and reached Albany at dusk, having completed about two thirds of the journey! He stayed with some friends, and then proceeded to his destination at daybreak the next day. It was an agonisingly slow trip, and he mistakenly thought to speed things up by putting the tractor into "angel gear" at the top of a long downhill run! Riding the bouncing runaway tractor downhill at a terrifying speed with the header behind, towering above him, swaying and bucking and threatening to tip over certainly added several years to his life!! I was not too impressed on hearing of that foolhardy experiment, thinking that I might have become a widow with four children and a fifth one due anytime!

The three boys camped in shearers' quarters on the two farms, working up and seeding the land in both Ongerup and Gairdner River, East of Albany. The three of them often kept the machinery operating 24 hours at a time, each doing 12-hour shifts. They worked out a 12-hour shift from 12 midday to 12 midnight, or 12 midnight to 12 midday, which seemed the best way of splitting it up as it gave them all the relief of some daylight hours as well as working under lights. Ploughing, harrowing and seeding the crops very often kept the machinery going constantly and this proved the most effective way of getting it done. Food was pretty basic as prepared by them, and sleep on mattresses on the floor in one room was a trial, especially when occasionally shared with the snorer of the family! Then the boys would return in early January to repeat that process to harvest the crop.

There was no tall timber as at Boyup Brook and so it was more open country with vistas over areas in crop under a huge expanse of sky. A mass of bright yellow in the spring when the canola crop was in flower, or acres of low green crop where wheat, oats and some barley was sown, turning into golden rippling acreages in the summer before harvest. When the land was being worked up and sown in the autumn the big machinery worked day and night preparing the ground and sowing the crops, with a light blue haze and smell of smoke pervading the area as sticks and stumps were being burnt. The hum of harvesters in the early summer also signalled the round-the-clock activity as the crops were taken off and filled the truck bins to be transported to the nearest grain handling bulk storage for eventual trucking to the ports and then shipment to their foreign destinations.

There was not much to stop the Easterly winds blowing in from the Nullarbor desert or down from the Northern wheat belt, bitterly cold in the night and early morning shifts on the tractors. Then stinking hot in the middle of the summer with hot winds and very dusty conditions. Those were the days before cabs on tractors and fully enclosed air-conditioned cabs on self-propelled harvesters. The heat, dust, flies and the itchiness of oats in particular, accompanied the operators of the farm machinery each and every day! Ploughing and seeding in the late autumn meant several layers of clothing; then overalls, topped with thickly layered jackets lined with wool or fur, fur lined gloves and woollen beanies! Mark had his father-in-law's flying jacket which proved very warm for these night operations!

As a means to an end the sharecropping proved an invaluable extra source of income, but we eventually gave away the share cropping at Ongerup after just the one year as wheat quotas had come in, as so many farmers had reduced their stocking rates so severely and had switched to growing wheat. We then concentrated just on the lighter land, South of Ongerup. This Gairdner River area was known as Mallee country - low scrubby trees with a big root system. These roots proved a great source for excellent firewood. Naturally there was the usual native scrub, but it had all been cleared and we just had to work up the country, seed the crop, and do a certain amount of picking up and burning of the inevitable debris that was turned up by the machinery. The handwork of picking up roots and burning them was basically done by Mum and Dad as the three brothers kept the tractors going as much as possible, and I was still in Boyup Brook, basically looking after that end, bringing up our family and expecting the fifth baby.

Cape Riche

Meanwhile we had discovered the State Government was releasing some land on the South coast of WA, about 100 miles east of Albany. We applied for a block of this virgin land in a roughly 22 inch per annum rainfall area. We were allocated 3000 acres with the proviso of clearing, fencing and bringing into production the minimum of 250 acres per year. Hence the "conditional purchase" title which meant that a total of 700 to 800 acres, cleared and fenced, of the 3000 acres had to be achieved before freehold was granted. The attraction to us was that the clearing was much lighter and therefore less expensive and quicker to bring in than the heavily timbered country at Boyup Brook. This would allow us to expand our total acreage, thereby creating more income for the family Ardua enterprise.

Cape Riche as the area was called was slightly undulating, basically sandy soiled, with some stunted Jarrah (little more than 4 to 6 feet high). There was also some Mallee native scrub; a few paper barks (Melaleuca) where there was more swampy land, and gorse type native bushes. All much cheaper to clear.

The views were to die for, undulating country with the Stirlings, Porongorups and Many Peaks as a backdrop on the horizon, to the North of the farm. These are "mountains" in local terms and are quite solid and significant hills, with rocky outcrops, and various beautiful hues in the late evening light.

The rolling acreage to the South, dropped away through break-away country to the Southern Ocean, some 8 miles away, with some islands offshore. It is a very pretty coastline with breaking surf on beautiful white sandy beaches, but very cold for swimming even in the summertime.

They experienced quite a bit of wind so near to the South coast, but the attraction for Mum was the absence of the frosts that we had every winter up at Boyup Brook and therefore she looked forward to gardening with impunity! Also, Boyup Brook could be quite cold in July and August and by this time both Mum and Dad were starting to suffer with some rheumatics and arthritis – small wonder with their hard physical work under basic conditions to start with at Boyup Brook. The area was certainly an attractive spot in the summer, without the extreme heat that Boyup Brook could achieve – but there was a lot of wind! Anyhow they decided to move down to Cape Riche and eventually build their house there.

I think Keith had found Boyup Brook a bit confining with all the big trees and bush surrounding the boundaries of our farm and missed the more open vistas he had enjoyed in the North Island of New Zealand he was farming in and looked forward to the different landscape. As I have said it was also a chance for Paddy to join the family partnership which could not have happened with just the proceeds off our first farming venture. Basically, the plan was for Keith and Paddy to run the sharecropping, with Mark helping when needed, and that they would establish themselves down South to clear and seed Cape Riche and start to run sheep there.

Meanwhile Mark and I would run the Boyup Brook end of things. Of course, we had a huge overdraft there and so it was then decided that we would have to sell Boyup Brook and purchase a "soldier settlement" block with a basic house on it, in the Gairdner area where we were presently sharecropping. This would mean we could keep the total proceeds of our efforts there for our own use. The Bank granted us "bridging finance" (over and above the overdraft!) to cover our change of tack, since we had put the Boyup farm on the market. Mark and I of course had mixed feelings about our change of direction. It would have meant our children would have had to change schools and of course our family leave all our friends behind. Not a problem when I was young and we had changed habitations and schools each time my Dad was posted in the RAF, but a major uprooting from the way of life *we* had established in Australia through the years of hard labour and broken dreams. We actually thought we had sold the farm at one point. However, the sale fell through, and we continued working the farm and gradually managed to adjust our plans and hang on. So eventually the Bank relented on selling us up. But that was the end of our clearing at Boyup Brook, as Cape Riche was the priority, so we never did clear the remaining 400 acres. It turned out just as well that *our* move was never made as the annual rainfall in the sharecropping areas dropped dramatically after a few years and we would have struggled to keep up our flow of income as planned, as the crop yields were very much reduced.

The two bachelor brothers moved down to Cape Riche, camping in a tent at first until they had worked out where they would establish sheds to start with etcetera. The first shed that was then built was to provide living quarters for the two boys and the parents.

A big high shed was erected with metal trusses and corrugated iron with three bays for machinery and then the fourth bay for living in with the floor raised off the ground, meaning there was storage space underneath. There were two bedrooms and a kitchen/living area, and they were all to occupy this until each of the boys got married and put up their own abodes. Then Mum and Dad were in splendid isolation there until their house was finished. Eventually a separate small ablution shed was erected, at the rear of the building as a bathroom, with a toilet and running water off the roofs of the buildings. But once again more uncomfortable basic living for Mark's parents.

Not long after the Cape Riche block had been allocated to the family a bush fire came through the region and roughly 2000 acres on the property were burnt. This left scrub and isolated small trees standing as blackened sentinels against the undulating area of burnt knee-high vegetation. (Once more carrying out the soothsayer's prophecy of fire attracted to Dad?!)

Keith and Paddy immediately tried disc ploughing some of the burnt area as the whole scene had opened up and looked to be easier clearing than the virgin green country that had been left unburnt. However, the ground was extremely rough to go over with the normal tractor because of the debris, and there were no wire-armoured tyres available for protection against the spiky mallee roots. Consequently, they tried putting covers over second-hand tractor tyres, but even these became in short supply. So in the end they hired a crawler tractor pulling a heavy disc plough and ploughed a thousand acres of the burnt area. Then they themselves reploughed, stick raked and burnt about 500 acres. Of course, Mum was in her element as the windrows of sticks and roots had to be set alight and burnt up, so she was very happy!

They then sowed perennial ryegrass and Woogenellup clover as a basic pasture and later tried growing some oats that they harvested with their second-hand tractor-drawn header (harvester), to have some grain to feed out as an extra supplement to the sheep when needed. They had to bring in a minimum of

250 acres each year, with a certain amount of country fenced, to conform to the conditional purchase agreement. They did not have to clear and burn quite to the degree that we had had to at Boyup Brook, as they were not clover rolling or harvesting.

Cape Riche had a reasonably stable climate in those early years and the earlier breaks of season usually meant the pasture growth provided green sheep feed before we had it at Boyup Brook. However, one year they received 5 inches of rain in March which delayed the seeding of the new country that year.

Meanwhile wheat quotas had come in as the wool trade had become barely viable as so many people had turned to cropping and beef, and so the sharecropping at Gairdner River was given away altogether.

Several dams were put in and of course the inevitable building of a shearing shed; sheep yards and habitations.

Our Trip to Uk

Just before Paddy joined Keith at Cape Riche to develop that farm, he and his wife Jackie, with their new babe, came to stay at Boyup Brook to run the farm whilst Mark and I had an eight-week trip to the UK in June, courtesy of my parents. Paddy was helped by our eldest 14-year-old son Paul to sow the crop at Boyup, whilst Mark's parents had our two youngest children, Jill and Andrew, down at Cape Riche attending the school there. Our eldest daughter Anne stayed with Mark's cousin and wife in Perth and attended school there. Our second daughter Sarah stayed with our neighbours and continued her schooling in Boyup Brook with Paul.

This was our first trip back to the UK and we had a wonderful time including a caravan trip to the Continent with my parents. We enjoyed travelling around to catch up with relatives and friends and appreciated the softer beauty and variety of landscape within short distances in the UK. The dawn chorus of the birds and the long summer evenings in the UK are a big memory of that holiday; the attractive picture perfect little stone villages we passed through the Cotswolds and the purple clad hills and vistas of heather in my homeland Scotland brought about nostalgia and a recognition of our earlier years before emigrating to Australia.

I did not have much to do with farming in the UK before I went to Australia, apart from staying on my uncle's small croft in Scotland during World War II when we were evacuated to Aberdeenshire. We lived in a small village and my brother and I attended the local small village school there and visited the croft from time to time. I loved the long summer holidays from school when I gave my uncle some help during harvest. My memories are of stooking the oat crop after it was reaped and bound. Then balancing on the hay cart stacking the stooks for travel to the farmyard and building a big haystack from the ground up. I always loved being outside and so this holiday was the start of my eventual romance with farming. Alas, there always seemed to be a lot of black mud on farms in the UK in the winter, and so it was a pleasant surprise to find Australian farming in WA, especially sheep farming, was a lot drier!

I do remember thinking how easy the British farmers got it, with all their subsidies from the government! The number of people employed on a farm in the UK seemed big in contrast to the size and scale of farming in Australia where often a big acreage was run by one or two people – often just husband and wife - but of course employing extras at certain times for skilled jobs like shearing.

Our holiday was very special and we filled it to the brim with activity, but it made us realise how much we loved our life in Australia with the challenge and satisfaction of the farming there. The wide-open vistas of sky and land, with the reddish orange dirt brilliant against the dark green of the native bush below the unending blue sky. The countryside bursting into the green and gold of the wattle bushes in springtime; plus the feeling of freedom and the vastness of the Australian landscape had captured us forever. We realised Australia was our home where our roots and family now belonged.

Vehicles at Boyup 'Ardua'

The sky-blue Austin truck had gone down to Ardua Cape Riche with many loads of equipment and had stayed there. A Daihatsu ute had been bought to do the job of the truck at Boyup. I thought this was quite exciting and had visions in future of driving up North for Mark and myself to have a holiday! But then I discovered what a workhorse it was, rugged and four-wheel-drive, but with no comforts or soft suspension and cramped for a long road trip! However, it truly served its purpose carrying many bags of seed and superphosphate at cropping time; bags of feed oats and lupins fed out to the sheep and the many sheep and lambs confined in a metal frame that Mark welded up to fit on the back tray. "Donkey Daihatsu" well and truly earned its keep over many years.

Dad had purchased a new car that we could use occasionally, but when they moved to Cape Riche for most of the time a second-hand Holden ute (utility) was purchased for the Boyup Brook farm and joy of joy we could use that as our own vehicle! The gearstick was on the steering column and we had a bench seat. All seven of us could actually fit in this ute with a certain amount of stacking! Mark drove with one child standing alongside, then me alongside with the youngest between my legs and two on my left, one sitting forward and one standing behind. Finally, one lying on quite a large ledge at the back of the cab! We all somehow slotted in, seemingly breathing by rote! If the weather was warm the children could spread themselves on a couple of mattresses in the back of the ute and we could all breathe easier. In those early days a lot of farmers only had utes like us, which doubled up as the family car. It was also a sturdy, hard-working, multi-use vehicle which could transport fencing materials, bags of stockfeed, loads of wood and rocks - you name it - and animals secured by a metal frame slotted in on the back tray.

Of course, in this day and age of seat belts and more affluence with cars and people movers, this does not and could not happen, which is probably not a bad thing!

Lunch on Arrival at Ardua. Pictured left to right, Basil, Keith, Paddy and Hope. *Photo taken by Mark.*

First covered camping kitchen. We were unable to move into the "shack" which we named Buckingham Palace (shown rear right) as the owner was still occupying it.

Morning Tea in the shack "Buckingham Palace". Pictured left to right, Hope, Mark, Keith, and Basil and Mink the cat.
Acknowledgement: The West Australian Newspaper.

Paddock of standing dead ring barked trees, providing some native grass and clover for sheep to graze on. Timber to be bulldozed and burnt up.

Windrow Clearing in Windermere. Bulldozed clearing of native bush (once looked like the native bush in the background) and windrowed for burning up at the end of summer.

Shearing shed being constructed. Basil and Keith "flying high".

Trailer load of stick pickers. Pictured left to right, Keith, Mark, Joan, Anne, Paul, Hope and Basil.

Mark & Joan's 14ft caravan
(Buckingham Palace rear right – bedroom for 3 children)

Shearing at Ardua.

Next generation Paul, our eldest son, throwing a fleece for inspection on the wool table prior to pressing into wool bales during shearing.

Aerial view of Ardua. Left to right, woolshed, Mark and Joan's house (centre) and cottage, all built by Basil.

Mark & Joan by extended house

Hope and Basil building the white house at Cape Riche with uncleared farmland directly behind them with Stirling Ranges in the far background.

Cartoon of Basil's success with establishing RTC (Rural Traders Cooperative).

Acknowledgement: The West Australian Newspaper.

Mother-In-Law

No words can express the very deep affection, admiration and regard I have had for my mother-in-law over all the years I knew her. I was welcomed into the family firstly as a 14-year-old tennis player friend of Mark (the middle son) and then as his fiancée at Fontainebleau. Finally living with them all in the early development days of farming in Boyup Brook and eventually as a daughter in law with their five grandchildren. She was so much a part of who Dad was, supporting him all the way in their civilian life just as she did in the Service and rising to the challenge as much as he did.

When we got to the age of 50+ we both marvelled at how the two of them had basically enjoyed their retirement, living under such difficulties, working so physically hard at that age and onwards. Then to do some of it all again when they moved down to Cape Riche, once more living in a shed and with no proper toilet to start with.

Cape Riche Housing

This was a completely new area that was being thrown open by the government and most people lived in sheds there, adapted as living quarters to start with, just as they had originally in the Boyup Brook area and all-around Australia. Gradually as the area became cleared and established, mainly by couples with young families, basic houses started appearing on the landscape. A little store sold essential foodstuffs, as the nearest town of Albany was some one hundred miles away, and a small school was eventually built.

Keith the eldest son got married and to start with occupied a Nissan hut that a neighbouring farmer had vacated for the house he had built. Keith then eventually built his own house away from the shed set-up and gradually extended it as time and money permitted, using quite a bit of timber off the farm at Boyup Brook.

When the youngest son Paddy joined the farming partnership full-time, he purchased a transportable house and moved into that.

Dad meanwhile was occupied building his third house! They chose a house site up on a hill and at the far end of the farming block to the existing shed. They had a magnificent view of the Stirling Ranges in one direction and the ocean and islands off Cape Riche on the other. The site was selected for the views, with no thought about the distance from the other families on the farm and the existing amenities such as access to electricity, telephone and roads!

He again chose concrete blocks, and these were white in colour - hence the title of "The White House" as it became known as within the family and district. Once again he chose a tiled roof. Building materials had improved over the years and the metal mesh concreted into the pad was quicker to install than the metal rods which were painstakingly welded at Boyup Brook. The window lintels were a flat metal bar instead of the concrete boxed lintels as made for our house. Sadly, the Colourbond tin roofing and the electric drilled tech screws were not available in those days, which would have made the roofing operation so much quicker and cheaper. Of course he was more skilled at what he was doing, but a few years older, and eventually progress was further slowed down as he took on the job of General President of the WA Farmers' Union. This position entailed travelling backwards and forwards to Perth for two years. This meant he really had only the weekends when he was able to work on the building, so progress was slow. However, his tenacity endured, and this much bigger house was eventually finished, and they were able to enjoy it for a few years.

The White House

Once the White House was virtually finished, they moved in. Their daughter Bridget came over from New Zealand and the long-awaited day arrived when we all assembled for the dual birthdays. Dad was born on the 28th of February and Mum was the next day in a leap year (which was the 29th), but they usually celebrated their birthdays on the 28th of the month - unless of course it was in a leap year. (Dad's 50th birthday had been in a leap year, so that auspicious 50th had taken precedence over Mum's date!)

Equally as important was that it was the day when there was to be the grand opening of all the packing cases that had been here, there and everywhere for years and years! Dad had his book with the case numbers and tabulated contents to the ready – but the excitement got the better of us all and he could not keep up with us - and much to his laughing chagrin- in the end it was the ripping off the lids which won the day. Mum saw all her treasures that been packed away for about thirty years – half of which she had forgotten they had! Such an excited celebration and so special for us all and the New Zealand members of the family to be a part of.

They enjoyed living in the house for three years or so and had many visitors to see them comfortably ensconced there. Dad was pleased to see his fireplace in the lounge, into which he had put a lot of planning and heartache, worked extremely well. It made the room a very cosy and delightful place to be in, snug from the rain lashing the windows, and the cold wind howling outside in the winter!

Mum started yet another garden planting fruit trees and shrubs etc and moved her vegie garden up the hill to the White House. Here she could enjoy the fruits of her labours, without the frosts she experienced in Boyup Brook! They had put in a huge cement water tank to catch the rain off the roof of their house, and so she was in seventh heaven with running water for her new garden! They also kept a couple of cats up there as there were bound to be a few snakes in the natural bush around the house site. Indeed, one day she was pruning the passionfruit vine outside the kitchen window, when she nearly cut the head off a Tiger snake that was hidden in the foliage! Fortunately, the secateurs got the snake behind its head and across the throat and immobilised it in the vine until Dad came to her aid and killed it! All in a day's work for them both!

Rape (Canola) Seed

Meanwhile we decided to try growing rape seed (or canola as it is more genteelly named nowadays!) at Boyup Brook to try to boost the income.

It is a minute seed, even smaller than clover seed, and is very subject to shedding before harvesting if it is at all windy. Some canola seed processing plants had been started up in the State to process the seed into oil for domestic use, and there was also an avenue to export it from Albany, a port down on the Southern coast of WA some 150 miles from the farm at Boyup Brook. The method of taking the seed off was by direct harvesting at that time and it was subject to a certain amount of the seed shedding, but it was the only way to do it. Another complication was the moisture content in the seed. We ran into trouble with the seed gaining moisture overnight as it sat in the truck bin in the cool night air, or if the weather at the time was a bit humid. We once sent a truckload all the way to Albany only to find the moisture content had exceeded the limit on arrival! A costly exercise! So, we did not persist with this income experiment for any length of time.

Later, methods changed, and the canola crop is now often mown and swathed into windrows. After it has had time and the weather to dry out the windrows are then picked up by the harvester and threshed into the harvester bin. The canola seed is then transported in bulk to railhead or port in truck bins and is often stored in silos with fan driven air passing through the seed to dry it out.

We often met up and lunched with Mark's parents at a half-way roadhouse as they drove back to Cape Riche from Perth, and we were telling them about this idea of growing rapeseed before we had ventured into it. There were some rather horrified faces in the room as Dad (who suffered deafness from flying for years in open cockpits) announced in a booming voice for all to hear "so, we are going in for rape in a big way!"

Cyclone Alby
at BOYUP BROOK

In those early days of our farming landowners used to set the stubble alight after the grain had been harvested to eradicate the regrowth of weeds, enabling easier re-cultivation of the areas, preparatory to sowing another crop or seeding pasture the next season. This method is not practised so much these days as there is the machinery to either spray or turn back the weeds into the ground before reseeding.

A cyclone was forecast to be brewing up in the North of WA, as so often happened at the end of the summer. Usually, cyclones blew themselves out West over the Indian Ocean long before they came down the coast, breaking up into a rain- bearing depression if they did progress down as far as us.

It was in early autumn and many farmers had successfully burned off their stubbles preparatory to seeding, and these areas were seemingly all extinguished and safe many days before the cyclone forecast. However, in 1969 Cyclone Alby reformed over the land and was blown down the West coast, extending its ferocious winds inland for 100 miles or so.

Unfortunately the gale force winds whipped up the burnt areas reigniting the areas that seemingly were deemed to be out and safe. The whole town of Boyup Brook was then ringed by these self-ignited fires. The fuel dump at the edge of town was threatened, and town inhabitants were assembled on the town football oval by the River Blackwood, as fires were raging throughout the whole district, and the town itself looked as though it was going to be destroyed.

The main gale force winds came through about midnight, and whilst none of our stubbles were re-ignited, we were greeted by a scene of utter devastation the next morning. We could not get off the farm for a whole week as trees were uprooted; fences were down, roads impassable and power lines demolished. The power of Mother Nature at her most horrendous and devastating! Fortunately, that did not happen often.

Extra Income

We had taken over the running of the Boyup Brook enterprise. We were not bringing in any more country at Boyup as all our funds were directed towards Cape Riche where we were working towards bringing in 300 acres every year, as the sooner it all became productive and fenced the sooner we could gain freehold possession of the property. But times were tough as bank interest rates on our overdraft had gone up to 24% per annum, and so we all had to look to gain some extra income off-farm in the slightly less busy times!

Keith and his wife Georgie established some off-farm income in the Spring selling wildflower seeds, as he was then trying to build his house in stages. This entailed harvesting seeds from the flowering wildflower plants in the bush around the Cape Riche area and on the farm and selling the seeds around the State of WA. His wife was also a qualified midwife and had worked for years at the local hospital in Albany, some 100 miles away.

The youngest son Paddy had been working on different farms to gain experience and when he married he went up North to work on the mines for a while and his wife continued teaching in Perth. Then when they started a family they joined the family partnership at Cape Riche, put up a transportable house, and Jackie taught at the local primary school.

We started to have increased costs with one of our children having to go away to Perth to boarding school for the last two years of education. This of course increased our cost of living quite dramatically and so we both had to find off-farm part-time employment to supplement our income. I had always just worked on the farm, apart from those three months just before we got married, when I worked for a solicitor in Perth to make some extra income for setting up our caravan.

Mark started a seasonal part-time business of sheep husbandry in some of the winter months, travelling around the district to various farms. I took on school bus driving during the term time, and of course this work was extra to our job of managing the farm. The Australian government sets up contracts for school bus operators to supply these orange and green school buses throughout the country in the various Shires in each State. It is a marvellous service, and these buses of varied sizes cover miles bringing the children of all ages to school and returning them home at the end of the day. Our run started on our farm around 7am to get to school for the start of lessons at 8.45am, and then at 3:30 pm returning to our farm. A long day for the children especially in their early days of education, but they seemed to adapt.

My initial foray into bus driving was to get myself the thirty miles into Boyup Brook at no cost so that I could find some sort of work there for the day, before the return trip in the afternoon. I offered to do this on a part-time basis to give the permanent driver and owner of our bus run the chance to have the odd day off and was quite prepared to do it for very little pay! It would be ideal for me, as I would go out of the door with the children and come back with them as the bus run started at our farm gate!

Once in town I was prepared to do anything to start with and I got myself a contract to clean the local football clubrooms once a week. I did some gardening for some people; did some stick picking on farms near town and then during the apple picking season I spent so many days a week picking apples in a local orchard.

My employer then increased my wage and frequency of trips and when she sold the bus run to a local company running several school buses, I was offered and took over our run on a permanent basis. I was supplied with a small Datsun car to travel back to the farm during the day, work for four or five hours there and then return to the town to bring the bus home. As I had a better wage, I then selected just a couple of my jobs in town to continue with, so that I could always drive home at pressure periods on the farm. There was a lot of driving involved, as the bus run was longer than the straight thirty miles into town, as the route wound around lots of different farms, probably covering an extra thirty miles. Then driving home and back in the car added another sixty miles, but the roads were a lot emptier compared with driving in the UK!

I had to have a special licence with an annual medical test to drive school children, and a truck licence as the bus I drove was the size of a Bedford truck!

I had a lot of adventures over the years with trees across the road; kangaroos bouncing out in front of the bus; emus racing down the road alongside the bus and once a black cockatoo crashing into the windscreen and cracking it severely. Occasionally I would have a breakdown in the school bus and no mobile phones in those days! But usually someone would come along, or I was able to limp the bus to the next pickup point where a parent could help in the situation. I once had part of the exhaust of the bus trailing on the ground and I hopped out, found a loose bit of wire off a fence and was lying on the ground under the bus carrying out the repair when a car stopped and the driver asked me where the bus driver was. I was in shorts and a bit dishevelled, so I guess it was a pertinent question!

There was no air-conditioning or heating in those days, and the dust on the dirt roads came in and exited the same way through cracks in the bus body and chassis. It was pretty cold on a frosty morning but stinking hot on the afternoon run, when the outside temperature was 30°Centigrade plus. I blessed my father for having taught me to drive in an old Morris car with a crash gearbox, as the reserve bus I had to use sometimes when the regular bus broke down, had a crash gearbox! Of course, none of the buses had power steering or air conditioning!

Our family of five children all progressed through their early schooling years locally in Boyup Brook. It was amazing how little five-year-olds could cope with the long bus travel, starting with three days a week, but then enduring the five-day week when a year older. These young ones often slept on the return journey after a full day in the classroom, but they soon adapted to reading a book, playing games, or just enjoying the company of their friends. All the bus travellers soon accepted the journey as normal, and amused themselves quite well, although the noise level had to be adjusted sometimes!

Mind you, I did once look up in the interior mirror to see money changing hands between some older kids at the back of the bus. When I had stopped the bus to find out just what was going on, I was assured that the money exchanging hands during their game of "Two-up" would be returned to the original owners at the end of the bus journey! Needless to say, that game was stopped!

This bus driving proved to be a good source of income and there were additional benefits in that I could often bring back supplies for our farming operations in those days which you certainly could not carry on a school bus in later years! We also used to deliver the daily newspapers in the early days with one pupil being assigned to throw out the newspaper as we travelled past each farm.

We also had to save a lot of money running the farm as money was so tight in those days. So *we* had to do a lot of the crutching of the sheep, instead of employing a shearer, and I would often help Mark by taking one of the stands and using a hand piece. Later we purchased a crutching cradle which meant we did eliminate some of the heavy work of handling the sheep over the board. This meant we had to position the mobile yards to enable the sheep to run through relatively easily, to then be captured in a race and tipped on their backs onto a cradle for the crutching operation and then be dropped off to exit the yards. There was quite an art in getting the sheep to run into and around these yards, with bends at the correct angles so that they ran without seeing what lay further ahead of them and the sunlight had to be at the right height and angle to the sheep to keep the operation flowing smoothly. Quite an art, subject to trial and error sometimes!

Driving big mileage is just a fact of life in Australia. We liked to encourage our children to play sport as it proved a relief for them from the ever-present jobs and isolation on the farm, and for us too. Great friendships were formed over the years which have remained steadfast to this day. The district held their Australian Rules Football competition for boys on a Saturday morning and the girls' netball games were in the afternoon in Boyup Brook. Of course, we had to do the mileage into town, and if Mark was not too busy, he would come as well. It could seem a bit of a bind sometimes, having driven the school bus in and out of town all week, but the time spent with our children over our lifetime was very brief in the scheme of things.

Mark was a rugby player, but Australian Rules football was the nearest our boys could get to it! Dad did rudely call the game "Aerial Ping Pong", but he had to admit that it was played with the right-shaped ball! We have followed our boys over their years of playing it and really enjoy the non-stop flow of that game. We believe rugby has been ruined with the present scrum and stop/start rules that seem to monopolize it.

WA FARMERS Union

Dad had been approached to get involved in Liberal Federal politics and stand in a constituency some years before, but his involvement with politics whilst in the Air Force had tainted any desire to become involved to that degree! However, he did agree to become the General President of the West Australian Farmers Union for a couple of years. The wool scene was still diabolical Australia wide, with the meat industry also in a mess, particularly in WA. He did a lot of work to try to improve that and to expand markets overseas, particularly in the Middle East.

He was the first General President of the Farmers Union to make the position a full-time job. At that time, he only had a Holden farm utility, that is a vehicle with a bench front seat and an enclosed tray behind. A strong vehicle but not made for comfort. He would rise at 4:30 AM on a Monday morning to drive the 300 miles to Perth to open the office at 9 AM. He stayed with his youngest son Paddy and wife in Perth for four nights in the week and then at 5 PM on a Friday he would drive back to Cape Riche to work on the house all weekend then repeating it all over again on the Monday morning.

Following this gruelling programme Dad was often driving down from Perth after his week in the Farmers Union office late at night. One evening someone came up behind him, but did not pass, blinding Dad with his headlights on high beam for miles on end and making it very difficult for him to see the highway ahead. Eventually the car passed him with a police siren blaring and signalled him to stop. Dad drew into the side of the road and a young police officer accused him of frequently driving over the white lines in the middle-of-the-road and adjusting his speed constantly.

Dad immediately barked at him that he was blinded by the full beam of the headlights behind him, following him for miles on end, and demanded to know the officer's number and area of operation as he was going to make a complaint to his higher authority!

The officer very quickly withdrew his officious assertion and allowed Dad to proceed on his way. Dad's demeanour, as always, still very much demanded respect and immediate action!

The Farmers Union had many different sections in it such as meat, wheat and wool et cetera, and as General President he could attend the monthly meetings of each section, which he did on a regular basis as a means of informing himself on their deliberations and decisions. On one occasion he noticed that a particular item had been coming up regularly in the agenda for a long time, but no decision had been reached. It was yet again agreed that it be shelved to the next meeting! So, he asked for permission to make an observation.

He said "If I was running this meeting, I would lock the door and not let anyone leave until a decision on this item has been reached. This has been going on for months! "

In ten minutes a decision was made! Shades of the days of his RAF command!

This punishing programme went on for two years and then he made the decision to leave the Farmers Union in order to take on the mission of becoming the Founding Director of the Rural Traders' Cooperative (RTC), established in Perth, to improve the meat marketing scene throughout the State of WA. As has been said the whole trade was in dire straits and the debacle in the wool trade had also contributed to this. Farmers were desperate for the ability to (a) sell their meat, (b) make a profit and (c) achieve a market overseas, and the Cooperative was a very welcome and well supported venture by most WA farmers.

Many farmers were still going to the wall as the saleyard prices very often did not cover the saleyard costs and freight to market. Banks were foreclosing on their farming customers because of this plight in the wool trade and the meat marketing side of things.

A more comfortable second-hand car was purchased but it was still a full-time job and his travel programme to Perth was still as regular, but also entailed more travel, often flying to the Middle East to the Arab Emirates. This meant work on the White House was further delayed. Of course, when he returned to Cape Riche the building of the house claimed his full attention and efforts, so he was really working under quite a bit of stress.

Rural Traders' Cooperative

Dad then decided that the sheep industry needed help and support. He got together with some leading lights in the farming industry and they created the Rural Traders Cooperative (RTC)

The aim of RTC was to streamline the live sheep trade locally and more importantly export to the Middle East, enabling farmers to deal directly with the buyers and cutting out the costly exercise of dealing through a "middleman". Indeed, the plan was for a cool store to be established and paid for by the Arabs in Dubai, so as I said Dad was not only travelling often to Perth, but also flying over to the Middle East to set up this partnership. The WA sheep farmers embraced the cooperative idea by buying shares in the new company to establish and finance it, with the intention of extending it to the local sheep market over the years. Going direct from the farm gate to the overseas customer would prove to be very advantageous and profitable so the establishment of these new overseas markets, supporting direct delivery to the customer, promised to be very popular and most attractive to all parties concerned.

In the middle of this Mum was found to have a cancerous spot on one lung which necessitated an operation to remove it. Dad was due to fly on one of his overseas trips and delayed his departure to be with her for a week or so. Mum was very bitter about her cancer and she complained to the surgeon that she had never smoked in her life. He said, "My dear if you had smoked you would have been dead a long time ago!" But she had been subjected to smoke-filled Nissan huts when in the WAAFs at Biggin Hill during the war. She would at times have to go outside with eyes streaming and lean against a wall coughing her lungs out. So many people smoked during the war to keep the hunger pangs at bay and steady the nerves during the many bombing raids.

Alas a few months later the export side of the RTC plan started to falter and Dad suffered some severe setbacks to his vision and plans for the Company. He had spent so much time and effort flying to and fro to the Arab Emirates setting up the whole export operation and had a tremendous rapport with the Arabs who were well prepared to build the cool store there, and the deal was just about signed and sealed. Suffice to say an unbusinesslike decision was made by someone in RTC that upset the Arabs, devastating Dad, because the equanimity could not be restored.

It was then that Dad experienced the sad fact that he was in civilian life, and not still in the Air Force! He would happily have had the culprit court-martialled in another life, but he did not receive the support from the rest of the Board to sack the individual, and the misdemeanor was not seen to have been dealt with sufficiently by their unhappy partners. Consequently, the international side of things all fell through. All this involvement, hard work and bitter disappointment took a certain toll on his constitution. Even his superb optimism and indomitable spirit could not undo the damage to his health - and thence his stroke. The disappointment of this whole affair must have been huge for him and of course he was unable to fully communicate this to anyone as he lost his power of speech with the stroke.

RTC carried on, but with the export market lost it really became like all the other livestock and merchandise agricultural companies in WA. The value of farmers getting a more direct marketing source overseas, thereby reducing their costs and sharing in the profits, had basically disappeared.

Thank you to the WA Farmers Union for their acknowledgement of the contribution to Agriculture made by Sir Basil Embry.

Dad's Stroke

As I have said Dad had been burning the candle at both ends, travelling up and down to Perth from Cape Riche every week, 300 miles each way, and attending lengthy meetings when in Perth. Also making trips overseas to the Middle East, speaking with the Arabs trying to cement ongoing export markets for WA sheep in the "live sheep export trade" and endeavouring to bolster the local meat supply market for WA farmers. This involved a lot of travel and quite stressful setting up of meetings, both in WA and overseas, plus spending many hours sitting at the conference table. He admitted he frequently did not take all the medication he had been prescribed as it very often interfered with his scheduled programme and the meetings he had to attend, so he was both physically and mentally under a lot of stress at that time.

He and Mum came back from Perth to spend a night with us on the Boyup Brook farm, and he had a very relaxing day watching Mark play cricket, but at the meal in the evening he suddenly sprang up saying he was not feeling well, rubbing one arm, and we noticed his mouth had drooped on one side. We immediately packed him off to bed and rang the nearest doctor some 35 miles away. The doctor said it was better to leave him resting in bed, rather than drive through kangaroo country at that late hour, and to bring him in in the morning. Of course, in the morning he felt fine and Mark had quite an argument to get him into the car to be driven to see this doctor. He told him the episode was a warning - as though a hand had tightly compressed the blood flow in one arm and then fortunately released it. But it was a warning of an impending stroke, and he must be more diligent with his medication and slow down his pace of working. Not words that Dad had ever wanted to hear in his busy involved life.

The warning signs were there, but basically rejected and ignored, and the next episode was when he and Mum were up in Perth, and he had another warning. Even then he spent valuable time trying to do up the laces of his shoes - stubborn to the last - before he would get in the taxi which took him literally just round the corner to the nearby main heart hospital in Perth. But once there he had a full-blown stroke shortly after admittance. The stroke was on his right side and so he lost his speech and was paralysed down the whole right side of his body. We never thought he would come out of the hospital, but gradually he improved and was eventually moved to the rehabilitation hospital in Perth where he slowly got more improvement in his condition through monitoring and exercise. But of course, his speech was never regained, and his paralysis was permanent.

A friend of my in-laws lent Mum a very nice townhouse in the centre of Perth close to the rehabilitation hospital, and she patiently spent her days between the hospital and the townhouse; knitting, catching up with a few friends in Perth and enjoying visits from her grandchildren, some of whom were in Perth at boarding school at that time. It must have seemed like the days in the war to her all over again, when Dad was off on flying operations, and she was left wondering how he was going, whether she would ever see him again, or ever resume a normal life with him.

She always said that she wished he had died at the time of the stroke, as it was such a cruel blow for a man of his capabilities and temperament. But she also had his same fortitude and attitude in life. This was borne out in how she helped him with his disability and was eventually able to cope with his return home to Cape Riche which of course meant a lot to him. The family at Cape Riche were a tremendous support to them and Dad continued to improve slowly for a time and was able to walk slowly with a stick in the house, but always needed someone at his side.

Their very good friend from Melbourne, Ian McRitchie, rang Mum every day in the weeks following the stroke to find out how Dad was getting on and when he returned to Cape Riche and had gained more strength and cognizance Ian flew his aeroplane over to spend some time with them. He was dreadfully upset at Dad's loss of speech and devised a plan to try to shock his system into speech revival. He took him up in his Beechcraft plane, and even put Dad's uniform jacket on him, in the hopes of jolting his psyche into speech. The amazing thing was that Dad could fly the aeroplane, one armed of course, and greatly enjoyed the experience of being in the air again. One can only imagine the joy for him of being up in the sky flying once more with his great friend and wartime flying buddy. But sadly," the experiment" although hugely enjoyable, did not work and his speech did not return.

How blessed were we that his stroke did not affect his character, as happens with so many, and his sense of humour could always rise to the top, although looking a little wry at times? A further example of his strength of character that he'd carried with him all through his lonely escape months and the many tours of flying operations.

In the early days after his stroke, he was in a waterbed to give him more comfort and less pressure sores and Mum took great delight in sitting on it to show off its bouncy capabilities, much to the laughing chagrin of Dad getting bounced up and down! He had been a stickler for correct interpretation and factual references all his life, having quite frequently remonstrated with Mum as she tried to embellish the truth or did not report things quite as they were! "Hope, that is not quite correct my dear" he would say. But of course, now she had an absolute field day, and all Dad could do was shake his head, shrug his one good shoulder, and then just laugh!

We never thought that he would ever return to Cape Riche to live after his stroke, much less be brought up to stay at the Boyup Brook farm for a time. I had been putting some brick paving down on a small patio outside our house and had run out of bricks. Dad had built a new letterbox and placed it on brick pillars at the entrance to the farm and as I thought he would never again be back to Boyup I had replaced the bricks with rounds of wood and placed the big wooden letterbox on top. There was nothing wrong with his observation skills which proved as keen as ever. Dad spotted the cannibalisation of his letter box as soon as he was driven up the driveway and pointed with his good arm and made obvious derogatory noises! I had to confess that I was the culprit, and why, and he just roared with laughter!

Mum needed time out from her nursing duties with Dad. It was heavy work and she also had broken sleep every night. She arranged for him to go into the respite center attached to the local hospital in Albany for the first of her five-day breaks and came up to the Boyup Brook farm for a bit of R and R with us. On her return she was appalled to find that Dad's mental and physical condition had hugely regressed. He thought he was abandoned to a life with the inmates of the Centre, with older people there in worse condition than himself, and that he would never get out. Mum swore she would never do that to him again.

We had a small district hospital in Boyup Brook and so we devised a plan with our local doctor and nursing staff that he be brought up to Boyup; probably spend a few days with us on the farm, and then go into the hospital for a week or so. This then gave Mum the chance to travel up to Perth for a break with friends or stay with us on the farm enjoying the grandchildren and having a rest and undisturbed sleeps. We were very busy on the farm of course, and I also drove the school bus five days a week. Dad had to spend time in Boyup Brook at the hospital, but he understood and was happy with this arrangement. And the local doctor could give him a regular medical check and of course Dad knew a lot of the local people who came and went. Our kids would often walk up the hill from school and visit him at lunchtimes. We were also able to take him into Mass when he spent time with us and this meant a lot to him, as they were too far out of the local town Albany to go to church very often whilst living at Cape Riche.

Sometimes when Mum was away, I would give Dad his shower in the morning, using the wheelchair to move him around into a shower chair in the bathroom. I would dress him in preparation to going out to one of the paddocks where we were picking up sticks and lighting fires, prior to working up the soil. The aim was to drive out there and set him up in his wheelchair to oversee what was going on in this sixty-acre paddock. I would find a good spot halfway up the hill and he could overlook the whole operation, "King of all he surveyed!" Dad used to love it and often we would barbecue some chops and have lunch in the paddock where he obviously felt a part of what was going on. After his shower I had to put his paralysed arm in a sling. This was the shoulder that bore the brunt of the German guards' rifle butts, during one of his many escapes in France, after being shot down in 1940. Although this right shoulder was paralysed by the stroke Dad suffered a lot of pain in it, which seemed to me most unfair as it was useless, and hence the sling. He let me put the sling on and then just as I was ready to push him out to the car, he waved his hand at me and grinned! I had put the sling on the wrong arm - and he had let me do it!!

Dad survived his stroke for two and a half years.... It was extremely hard on Mum, and we were all unsure of how much longer she could keep going, with broken sleep every night; supporting his weight to help him move out of his bed; showering him and helping him move around the house. But it came as a tremendous shock the last time he came up to Boyup and into the hospital for his R and R when the doctor warned us that his system was starting to break down. Indeed, suddenly to such an extent that we sat up all that first night with the local priest because we really did not think he would last the night, only to see him sitting up in bed eating a boiled egg for breakfast the next morning! Mum returned straight away and for a day or two it was hard as his system went down at nighttime but then rallied during the day. His tough constitution and that indomitable spirit of his just would not give in. I never realised dying could be such hard work and take so long but I guess it was his will that had carried him through the war that would not be subdued or abandoned. He died around midnight on 7 December 1977. Our memories are still stirred by the sound of the mopawk owl (similar to a cuckoo's call) that echoed in that still night as we sadly drove home to the farm, and that we again hear sometimes in the moonlight.

Dad was buried in the little cemetery at Boyup Brook; on a peaceful hillside overlooking a vista of green countryside and farming land, that was so much a part of his initial foray into farming. Their very great friends Air Marshall Sir Wallace and Lady Molly Kyle drove down from Perth in their official State Governor's car. A lot of people from Perth joined the locals to farewell Air Chief Marshal Sir Basil Embry but there was no great pomp or ceremony. Just the simple coffin, draped with the flag of the Royal Air Force, with a small wreath of the NZ Christmas Bush on top, from his daughter in NZ, and a very stoic widow with her three sons by her side.

Looking up into the blue unending vista of sky - one could imagine a great cohort of his wartime flying buddies looking down and saying "Welcome Basil, we've been waiting for you! What took you so long?"

Mum after Dad Died

After Dad died Mum flew over to Britain to catch up with so many of her friends whom she had not seen or heard from for so many years. We can only imagine the heartfelt condolences expressed to her on Dad's sad last few years and his death. There must also have been many stories and much reminiscing on his Service life and his character throughout many years both in Britain and Australia.

On her return to Australia Mum acquiesced to the boys' idea of splitting up the farming partnership as all the brothers had families of differing ages and requirements. She very generously made this possible by agreeing to facilitate it relatively easily as the Cape Riche block was big enough to split in two, with Keith and Paddy retaining approximately 1500 acres each. The Boyup Brook entity for us was a slightly bigger 1600 acres in size, but virtually 1100 acres after taking out the area of wastage due to creeks and rocky areas.

Mum also gave us some money to finish off our house, demolishing the fibro wall and sloping tin roof that was over our existing kitchen/dining area. We were then able to add a lounge off that dining area, completing a tile roof over the whole area to marry up with the original roof, although sadly the roof tiles were not quite matching in colour. Keith and Paddy were also able to extend their abodes due to Mum's generosity and the boys secured Mum's home tenure by fencing off an area around the White House, separate to their farms.

Dad had been the Chairman of the RAF Benevolent Fund and had maintained a keen interest and involvement in the work of the Society for many years. After his death the members very generously made the offer to assist Mum in some way. They facilitated and paid for a small car for her to use as she was living about ten km away, at the far end of the farm from the two boys at Cape Riche. This then entailed some driving lessons for her as she had never really driven before. Reversing was a challenge and she solved it by saying "oh I am too old to do that!" However, she managed to obtain a" restricted licence," just to get down to the homes of the two boys and also fifteen kms or so down the minor road to the little store at Wellstead where she would go very occasionally to do some food shopping.

She still kept a keen interest in the farms and spent a lot of her time at Cape Riche burning up sticks and roots in the paddocks, digging out thistles and of course her veggie garden was still very productive and appreciated. She was driven up to Boyup Brook every 6 to 8 weeks or so to check on the growing grandchildren there and to see what we were up to on that farm. And again busied herself burning up, or in the veggie garden and mending articles of clothing for the grandchildren! They used to save up articles that needed repairing; holes to be patched or darned; buttons to be sewn on, and she always had her knitting with her. And of course her rock buns, biscuits and cakes were always popular too!

Meanwhile Mum's health was deteriorating. Windy weather caused her angina to arc up and her breathing was often severely affected which eventually meant she experienced some heart problems. On one of her visits to Boyup Brook she ended up in the local hospital where they had to resuscitate her. They then sent her through to one of the Perth Hospitals in a Royal Flying Doctor plane. We pulled her leg at going to such lengths to have another flight! After a week or two Mum returned to Cape Riche and then Paddy added a room onto his house for her and she moved down from the White House to live with them.

She still came up to Boyup Brook for brief visits and it was literally the night before one such visit, when she was to be flown up by a Cape Riche neighbour in his small aeroplane, that her heart gave out and she suddenly died in her sleep on March 28th 1985. She would have been very cross at missing out on her flight! Although it came as a big shock to us all we were so glad that she had such a quick and peaceful ending, as she had frequently suffered dreadfully from breathlessness and heart pain at the end of each day.

She was of Scottish descent and had always threatened that she would come back and haunt us if a lot of money was spent on her burial and if she was transported back to Boyup Brook to be buried beside Dad! Her choice had been cremation, but as there was no crematorium nearer than about 200 miles away and bearing in her mind her aversion to spending any more funds than necessary, it was decided to respect her wishes and have a short graveside service and burial in the Albany cemetery. So that is where Lady Margaret Mildred Norfolk Hope Embry was laid to rest.

ARDUA BOYUP BROOK

Once the sharecropping down South was cut back a bit and so obviously easier for the "local" brothers at Cape Riche to do, Mark concentrated most of his time and efforts at Boyup Brook. We no longer clover rolled and ran more sheep on the farm and only cropped a smaller area each year. We were growing some grain for marketing but basically to harvest and store in the three grain silos that we had built, to then feed out to our sheep at the break of season when the green feed had not come away enough. Mark worked up the land and sowed the crops and we employed a contract harvester to take the grain off, trucking and auguring it into the silos we had installed.

We did the inevitable handwork, stacking and burning up of the roots and stumps that inexorably were exposed each year by the implements used to prepare the country for seeding. We also still had the soul-destroying chore of rock picking in the paddocks where there were some ironstone or granite rocks which would have proved detrimental to the harvester. Our small Ford Dexta tractor had a bucket on the front on hydraulics and one of us would drive whilst the other would walk in front and toss the rocks in, and then at the tip of a lever would drop the load on a rocky outcrop. A test for any marriage! I used to imagine it was like being a convict and was my least favourite job. At least heaping up sticks, stumps and roots in a heap, we then got rid of them by lighting a fire! I still enjoy burning up - the smell of the gum and the smoke in the burning wood and the satisfaction of clearing up a mess on the ground. Just as I loved the smell of the soil being worked up and seeing the different soil types in a variety of colours, with the sense of quiet achievement as the final paddock was sown.

This was a busy time to get the crop in whilst the soil was still warm and damp at the break of the season, so of course we welcomed the additional workforce at the weekends and during the school holidays when the kids were at home. It was very evident over the years that kids like ours off farms around us were basically very self-reliant and used to working physically from a very early age. They also learnt to drive very proficiently and safely, with lots of practice in the confines of a wide-open paddock! But it wasn't all slave driving and hard work though, as we had barbecues out in the paddock at lunchtime or we would break up the monotony with the promise of "Balga burning" that evening.

All our five children exercised their special skills with us on the farm and were of tremendous help as they grew up - in the woolshed; sheep yards; feeding out to sheep and at lamb-marking time, and generally lending a hand on whatever jobs we were involved in over the years.

One enduring memory I have is of the noisy yellow Chamberlain tractor driven by Sarah with one of the farm dogs beside her on the bench seat and then her older sister Anne reading a book - as they went round and round the paddock pulling the plough. Both girls were rugged up with scarves and beanies in the cold weather!

We had a 100-acre block of natural bush which we called "the swamp block" with some huge Red Gum trees on it and with a natural spring dam, beautiful to swim in until we discovered leeches, and they discovered us! This block had a lot of these Balga trees that I spoke of earlier. We would go along after nightfall and strike a match to hold it to the fringe of one of these 4 to 6ft trees. The flame easily caught alight on the straw-like material or fronds hanging down to head height and flared up quickly travelling to the top of the tree. The art of this activity was to then grab a bunch of these fronds, light them and then run around as though holding an Olympic torch lighting up the fringes of other Balga trees, illuminating the scene in a very spectacular fashion - better than any firework display and lighting up the surrounds and creating warmth for us all very quickly. The black gum-filled trunks and tops of these trees exuded a beautiful pungent smoke that had a peculiar and iconic scent that remains in one's memory and evokes much wistfulness each time I experience it to this day. It does not sound possible; but the amazing thing is that this does the Balga no harm at all, just refreshing its top to produce fresh growth for the next season, as it is basically the fringe that burns and not the trunks. This was also a very favourite attraction for any of our visitors to the farm, but not of course in the heat and dryness of the summer!!

The stick picking caper was also an attractive activity for our visitors, and we got through a lot of work loading the tip trailer and then offloading on heaps and setting them alight. I think they thought it was a great fun activity and how lucky were we to "live it" all the time. But there were lots of jobs on the farm that were not fun activities!

Actually, I sometimes look back on those years on the farm - from the very beginning - and think how much of that soil and land *we all* had walked and worked over. All those pad-docks, from clearing virgin "green native bush"; to working up land under cultivation; to growing a crop; to droving sheep, heavy in wool through a lush green grassy paddock, or lighting up the crop stubble in a running fire preparatory to sowing another crop. We must have trodden on just about every inch of that soil over all those years! Not a bad effort for an Air Chief Marshal, used to winging it through the clouds - but I guess such a contrast to those hectic, desperate wartime days!

Latter Years of Ardua

The years passed very quickly with the work on the farm being so seasonal, and one season seemed to blend into the next.

Looking back over the years we had been very fortunate to welcome my parents over to WA numerous times, and in later years, in their retirement.

When they visited, they had the cottage at Boyup all to themselves, after Mark's parents had moved down to the Cape Riche farm, and so could retreat up there when the exuberant noise in our house became too much for them!

They got to know our children really well over the years on these many trips to WA. Our eldest daughter Anne stayed with them for a few months in the UK and they took her to France in their caravan for a holiday. Our youngest daughter Jill worked as a roustabout with a mobile shearing and sheep-dipping team in England in her late teens and she and Colin spent quite a bit of downtime with them too.

One of my parents' trips was to attend the three weddings of Jill, Paul, and Sarah - who brought her wedding date forward - so that they would still be able to attend that one too before their return date to the UK! We had three weddings within three months, with Christmas and some birthdays in between – just to keep the party mood going over the time! We all suffered withdrawal symptoms at the end of it all!

So although my parents had missed out on my early years of farming out in Australia, they got to experience some of the challenges, highs, lows and rewards that inevitably accompanied our pioneering lifestyle on their various visits over the years. They also greatly enjoyed meeting seven of their great grandchildren on their last trip!

This was not afforded to Mark's parents who sadly were not alive to know all our children as adults and meet and know the excellent partners they have all chosen in life. What a happy bunch they are and how well they all get on with each other. We are very blessed!

Our family had grown up and taken off on various missions in life. Our eldest son came back on the farm but had to get the majority of his income off- farm to start with for a good few years. He learnt to shear sheep which was very hard work but quite well paid and also supplemented his Ardua income by taking over some of the school bus driving from me, except at pressure times on farm. He mostly did just the morning run which conflicted less with the farm work, and I would do the afternoon trip. I quite missed the morning run as when it was frosty I thought it was quite like driving through fairyland as the bus descended into gullies over small creeks with the frost glinting and sparkling on the branches and leaves. Well worth seeing despite the drop in temperature and the early start! Also, the schoolkids were quieter and better behaved, whereas in the afternoons they were inclined to be more noisy, happy to be released for the day!

Paul got married and he and Melodie bought a house in Perth that was then cut in half and transported onsite, near enough to hook on to the electricity, but giving all of us plenty of space! Eventually he took over the running of Ardua Boyup Brook and we semi-retired to Dunsborough where we now live.

We had always spent two weeks there with our family on our annual holiday for years, enjoying an idyllic two weeks, swimming and relaxing, and in the latter years sailing, golfing and sussing out the local wineries!

The bus driving contract was relinquished after 15 years of running it and we only returned to the farm at pressure times, but gradually we became superfluous to the workload there as Paul and his wife took over the whole scene. It was a wrench to leave Mark's two sheep dogs behind, but Paul needed them, and it would have been unkind to have submitted them to a relatively small back garden – but they did look at us very reproachfully each time we got into the car and returned to Dunsborough!

Sheep and wool prices were fairly ordinary and so Paul decided to plant a vineyard to diversify his income and we assured him that we and many of our friends would support him with our purchase and consumption of wine! However, after a few years the bottom dropped out of the wine industry to a degree; the price of superphosphate fertiliser doubled in price and Paul suffered high blood pressure with other problems related to stress - so the decision was made to sell the farm.

That was not an easy decision as Paul was only too aware of the history and sacrifices made over the years and had shared in them as had all our children. However, our neighbour, originally from Norfolk in England, bought the farm and so the history of farming the land is continuing. Many farmers in the district were selling their farms at that stage; or buying up farms alongside or near their properties, or planting trees to diversify their incomes. This has been a sad state of affairs, as the number of families farming in many areas has diminished somewhat. This then has had a negative impact on school sizes and businesses in the small towns, as the population decreased. Costs had gone up, but farm incomes hadn't, so it was a case of getting a bigger acreage or creating an alternative income.

Ardua was then bought by our neighbours who continued to farm it. We were so glad that it was not planted with quick growing Tasmanian Blue Gums to be exported to the Far East as wood chips, as I think Mum and Dad would have turned in their graves to see a forest of trees on the cleared land after all our hard work and sacrifices over the years! And we certainly felt that way too!

The planting of Tasmanian Blue Gums has given many farmers an opportunity to diversify their income and obtain a quick return on some areas on their farm. Many of the older farmers who were finding the physical activity needed to run a farm was becoming harder, chose to plant some trees to supplement their income off the land. Many of the younger generation were no longer attracted to the farming life as the monetary return was no longer there to compensate for all the hard work and effort involved. Many people in the State were sinking their savings into investment companies who promised big returns on this timber exported offshore on ships from the ports around WA. There was a big demand for land to plant these gum trees on, so sadly there were many farms that went into these Tasmanian Blue Gums, and who could blame them.

The trees were reasonably quick growing, and the first cut could be after five years in the ground, followed by a second cut a few years later. The wool trade was still in the doldrums and cattle prices were mediocre. However, we found it very depressing to see good farming areas under these eucalypts, blocking the rolling views we used to enjoy in our area and of course as I said, affecting the viability and facilities in the local district.

However, the timber growing is no longer continuing so much in the district and many areas are now being re-cleared and opened up to farming, having gone the full circle. Massive new equipment imported from the USA is now being contracted to rip out all the stumps, so the land and rolling countryside is now being exposed again to sheep, cattle and arable farming - which is a joy to see!

Retirement

I had first sailed with my father when I was 16 and we used to drive down to Chichester from the suburb we lived in near London to sail in the yachts that the RAF kept at RAF Thorney Island. When my Dad was posted to the 2nd TAF in Germany I used to continue sailing on a big lake near Hanover, but I never thought it would happen again farming and living inland from the sea in Western Australia.

However, our annual holidays by the sea renewed the desire for a yacht and to start with we bought a little Mirror sailing dinghy. None of the family were interested in sailing but we loved it and when we saw a bigger yacht for sale in Boyup Brook of all places, we could not resist it! We had a good wool cheque that year and it was a red boat that we had visualised having over the years! We could only use this yacht on our annual fortnight's holiday off the farm and so trailered it down South every year. When our friends from Perth visited the farm, we used to have drinks on board the yacht on the trailer in the evening, climbing aboard and admiring the sunset as the afterglow lit up the hills and trees around us, with the peace and harmony of the magpies and little birds chorusing in the evening dusk.

In retirement we did the same thing, anchored on our buoy, surveying the ever-changing scene and the setting sun with all the beautiful colours, the peaceful lap of water on the hull and with a glass of wine in our hands! Not an experience to be swapped for anything! We used to wonder what the rich people were doing - as we reckoned we had the best of everything and not to be swapped for all the money in China!

We up-sized yachts twice and the final one was bigger for more comfort but for us both to still manage, that we could sleep on and live on to travel further afield. We justified the upgrade because interest rates on the money in our bank balance were minimal, and we reasoned the pleasure we would get from our purchase would far outweigh the meagre interest we would receive on our bank balance!

We spent quite a bit of time in Malaysia for a few years, sharing a condominium with three other Australians and made many Malaysian friends over there, greatly enjoying their sense of humour. But we were always glad to return to WA and our first port of call would be to go to a big lookout and breathe in the fresh air and enjoy the vista of sea and sky over the rolling Indian Ocean.

Looking back on *our* farming life and discussing the constant varying challenges we faced, and the hard work and pauper existence we had for many years, our biggest regret was that we had no independence for so long. We didn't have a car and so everyone knew where we were going, for so many years. It doesn't sound much, and we could always borrow a car, but had to have it back by a certain time. And farming in a family partnership had its challenges for all of us.

Possibly Dad could have bought land where there was lighter clearing; where there was a house and basic sheds to start with and where more land was cleared and productive. The possibilities are endless. But on looking back Ardua

Boyup Brook was exactly the sort of challenge he was looking for and needed, to replace those hectic war years and his love of flying.

And our one consolation was that it was character building - for all of us!

Ending

I often wonder what Dad would think of the world now. So many lives lost - so many friends gone, and to what end? And what does the future now hold for the growing number of his offspring - his great, great grandchildren?

He would be sad for the country where he was born, flew above and fought for during the war. So much red tape; political correctness; curtailment of free thinking and degradation of Christian beliefs and values - and now the overwhelming challenge of Covid worldwide and war.

Then the Australia that he was attracted to through his contact with his many flying buddies during wartime and where he chose to settle on his retirement. He would not have settled for the easy acceptance of a government pandering to today's minority groups and a population whose social and Christian values are discarded in the name of equality and social justice.

But then I console myself with the knowledge that he accepted and indeed always looked for a challenging life. In Australia he was following the adventure of 20th century pioneering and gave all his immediate family and now his descendants, the examples of hard work, good humour, belief in self and family, governed by practical, lived-out Christian values.

Our five adult children
(LtoR Andrew, Jill, Sarah, Anne & Paul)

Mark & Joan sailing in retirement